Lives of Crime & Other Stories

Texture Press
Managing Editor: Susan Smith Nash, Ph.D.
1108 Westbrooke Terrace
Norman, OK 73072
E-mail: texturepress@beyondutopia.com

Cover design by Arlene Ang
Cover based on the "The Loveless Cafe" by Mike Stanko, used by permission
Interior design by Texture Press
Author photograph by Michael George, used by permission

ISBN-13: 978-0692300039
ISBN-10: 0692300031

Lives of Crime & Other Stories

L. Shapley Bassen

2014

Texture Press
Norman, Oklahoma

Dedication

To all the characters herein

For facing their two mirrors up to nature

Table of Contents

Lives of Crime

The hammer was still stuck into the old jeweler's brow and he was alive when Ryan arrived. EMS was right behind him. By the time the sirens had wailed the victim away into the winter night, his son had calmed down enough to answer questions. Ryan saw the middle-aged man was simple. He spoke in chopped sentences, couldn't focus, but not like someone in shock; like someone who never could. All Ryan could get from him was that it was about rubies. "Not the good ones." That detail disturbed the short, overweight man far more than the hammer in his father's forehead or that he'd been an eyewitness, close enough to have his father's blood spattered on his white shirt. However, he was more useful than the unconscious victim or his hysterical wife, a wailing, short woman named Minnie who kept repeating her husband's name in Yiddish until she'd been carted away with him in the ambulance. Those EMTs earned their money.

It was a routine armed robbery except for the hammer. Ryan had been handed the routine cases since his wife Eileen, also a cop, had been killed in the line of duty eight months earlier, which had left Ryan with a six-year-old son to raise. The PBA had a good deal, paying half the housekeeper cost and finding a woman to come in to take care of Sean after school. Maryrose Magro also lived in Jackson Heights. She could pick Sean up at the school door beside the other mothers with strollers. Maryrose had a stroller of her own, with a two-year-old girl in it.

Ryan wasn't going to get any more information from the jeweler's simple son. The robbery was similar to four others that had taken place within the past six weeks in the same area of south Queens, some of them house break-ins. This was the first violence on the familiar MO. Ryan knew the guy from enough descriptions: white, late twenties, dark blue windbreaker. He must be cold and shivering in this weather. He had ripped off a deli under the new ownership of one of the many Koreans moving into this outer borough of 1970s NYC. First a liquor store, now the jeweler. "He got out of the camps," the son had whimpered. Ryan figured the tough old Jew had resisted. That kid was just one more Nazi to him. The jeweler gave him some cash and cloudy rubies. *Cabochons*, Ryan remembered they were called.

Maryrose was twenty-three, married to a high school Social Studies teacher named Tony, who was Ryan's age – thirty-five. Maryrose had been Tony's student at Bayside High School. She had been a very good student, accepted at Queens College and even Hunter in the city, but she came from a cracked family with no time or money for Maryrose, so she got a job as a teacher's aide at Bayside. One thing led to another. Married two years later at twenty, Maryrose had a two-year-old girl by the time she was twenty-three.

Ryan hadn't made a move toward her; if he lost her, it would hurt Sean. The night of the hammer robbery, Ryan got in late. He watched Maryrose giving Sean a bath. Her little girl was already asleep in the living room of the apartment in the portacrib he'd set up for her there.

Sean was singing a song he'd learned at school, something about *March winds blowing, May bringing us flowers.* It wasn't March yet, just February, with blizzard warnings announced at quarter hour intervals by hysterical weather reporters on radio and TV. Ryan stood in the bathroom doorway, watching Maryrose soap down Sean's back, shampoo his straight blond hair, like Eileen's, up into a point on the top of his head. Sean laughed and dived into the bath suds. He popped out of the water and stood up, hugging Maryrose. "I love you!"

The intensity of the child's emotion stiffened Ryan. Maryrose surrounded the boy in a towel and hefted him out of the tub. "You'd better get out before you're all wrinkles." Ryan saw where Sean's wetness had pressed against her so that the outline of her bra, her nipples, and the full curve of her breasts were bared to him. He walked away.

In the kitchen, Ryan was taking a long swallow of warm beer

straight from the six-pack next to the refrigerator. Maryrose followed the towel-swathed Sean.

"Gonna snow," Sean announced.

"Maybe you'll get a day off from school. You're leaving wet footprints on the floor."

"So you can follow my tracks."

Maryrose said, "Sean belongs in bed and I belong home before the storm hits."

Sean grabbed Maryrose's hand. "I want her to put me to bed!"

As she led the child down the hall, Ryan silently agreed with his son. It wasn't just about getting laid. He'd gone to Terese, a cop in his precinct. Ryan liked Terese and she wasn't ugly. She was divorced and not interested in the past or future. Terese hadn't come to Eileen's funeral but a week later she stopped at the apartment and told Ryan when he wanted it, just to come to her, he was a nice-looking guy and Eileen had always said for her to look out for him if anything happened. On that summer day, Ryan had no appetite. Later on, it came back to him, and they had a good time, like the day before yesterday, so it wasn't sex. It was Maryrose.

He followed her to Sean's bedroom and again leaned against the doorjamb, listening to her prompt Sean in his prayers and then sing a lullaby. In a light but steady voice, she carried the old tune his grandmother had also sung to him about a Japanese sandman. Ryan went to the living room window behind the couch. The snow had started. He opened the sheer white curtains. He couldn't see to the streetlight on the near corner.

Maryrose returned to the living room and went to the portacrib where her little girl was sleeping, thumb in mouth. The child looked like her. Eileen called women like Maryrose *meatloaf,* as much for their domestic nature as their shape.

He gestured, "You going to take the baby out in this?"

"Tony is going to want us home."

Ryan felt hypnotized by the snow. He could hear Maryrose in the kitchen making a phone call. He heard her slam down the receiver. He went into the kitchen and took another warm beer.

"You never ate. Sit down."

Ryan ate the pot roast she'd kept warm with mashed potatoes, and a still crisp salad she took from the refrigerator. She poured the beer into a glass for him and handed him a napkin. Neither of them spoke; the storm roared, mauling the building. When he finished eating, Ryan took his dishes to the sink. Maryrose turned, ready to wash them.

"You're tired. Watch TV in my room. Fall asleep."

Her face asked the question, but Ryan looked down and washed his dishes. After, though it wasn't late, he felt beat. He turned out the lights in the living room, checked Maryrose's baby once, and lay down on the couch. He covered his eyes with his arm, pulled the crocheted afghan over him and sank into the dark.

Maybe it was a strong gust; Ryan bolted awake, sitting up on the couch, uncomfortable in his clothes, both chilled and sweaty. The blizzard bellowed outdoors. How many lives would this storm take? It was going to be a mess in the morning driving to Maspeth, maybe two feet of snow on these Queens roads, the last to be plowed out if you didn't count Staten Island, which everyone didn't. If you lived in Staten Island, you'd turned your back on a city glad to return the gesture with both arm and finger. The snow could slow down Ryan's neat-thief, but finding the fence with the cabochon rubies would also be—

At first, Ryan thought he saw the white gauze curtains billow, but there wasn't enough of a crack anywhere around the windows to cause that. Then the phone rang. Ryan rushed to the kitchen to pick it up before it might wake the children or Maryrose. It was the precinct; the jeweler had died.

"You couldn't wait till morning to tell me?" Ryan demanded then apologized because he'd left instructions to be informed immediately if it had been upped to homicide so he'd know who'd be assigned. He hung up the phone and walked back into the dark living room.

He saw the jeweler standing there, holding in his up-turned palm a handful of rubies. Ryan froze. The jeweler tilted his dented head and turned his hand so that the rubies fell in a red column to the carpeted floor. Ryan's eyes followed the falling stones; when he looked up, the jeweler was gone.

His heart thudded in rhythm to the storm's pounding. He tried to time it, like thunder after lightning. There was a scent of ozone and he felt dizzy. A stroke? Maryrose appeared in the archway from the hall. She was real. She was wearing the red-striped pajamas Eileen had given him. They were too big for her.

"Did the baby wake you?" She padded over to the portacrib and tucked the quilt around her child.

"It was the phone. Guy died."

"I can't sleep anyway."

"Do you believe in ghosts?"

"You look like one. Are you all right?"

Ryan was shocked when he groaned. He took Maryrose in his arms and held onto her. She was warm, heavy and soft. He felt her heart pulse. She patted his back like a baby's.

"I didn't know cops took it so personally," Maryrose whispered, "but I guess you must, sometimes."

He looked down into her plain face, into brown eyes that caught whatever snowy light there was. Ryan shut his own eyes and leaned into a kiss she accepted then returned. He put his hand on the back of her head and held her, deepening the kiss into sexual demand, and still Maryrose allowed it, opening her mouth wider to him, welcoming him in. He groaned again. In his bed, he hid inside her and she covered him. Later, as dawn dimly began, they echoed the utter silence after the storm.

"Thank you," Ryan whispered.

Maryrose laughed. Ryan thought of the falling rubies.

Out of the shower, he walked into the living room wearing a terrycloth robe. Sean was on the floor, moving Transformers toward the two-year-old's crib where she was sitting up, happily screaming through the thumb still in her mouth as his son threatened her with pretend-monster toys. Sean saw his father and joyfully reported, "Snow day, Daddy, snow day the radio said!" The white curtains were pulled back and revealed over apartment rooftops the dazzling view of heaven the aftermath of a blizzard sometimes allows even in Queens.

The door buzzed. Maryrose, dressed, hair back in ponytail, answered it. At the same moment, Sean saw something in the carpet, scooped it up in his small hands, and said, "Look, Daddy!"

Tony Magro was at the door, snow caked up to his knees. He looked sleepy and worried. He lifted his eager little girl up out of the portacrib. Ryan opened his hand to accept Sean's discovery. For a moment, it looked like round, cloudy stones, but when he closed his palm, it felt like dried mud and disintegrated into dust as it drifted back to the floor.

"You have to go out in this? Magro asked. "Interesting case?"

Ryan looked out the window at the snowy Wonderland; the teacher had the day off.

"Somebody stole rubies," Maryrose said.

"You think you'll find him – or them?"

He asks too many questions, Ryan thought, but thank god they were the wrong ones.

A Cultural Revolution

Ti Chi Wing is on a journey. This is his first departure from home and family in Canton, and he would feel better about it if his sister Lang is not also on another dusty bus traveling northeast. Chi Wing travels northwest to Gansu, below the Mongolian border. As he boards the bus, his mother reminds him of Confucius' day when scholars are sent into the backwaters of the empire. Their rise in the bureaucracy is as much determined by calligraphy and poetry as office skills. Chi Wing's mother thinks Confucius is a wise man for affirming the causal relationship between art and power. His professor father is absent; he is confined at home in disgrace.

Chi Wing is on the bus with classmates. There is little talk. Chi Wing looks out the dirty window at countryside. Learning about farming is interesting. It is a course in botany. The commune in Gansu is another country. A deep scolding voice approaches. They are led to a long one story stone building. The unpainted blocks have few windows. A windmill turns at one corner of the commune. Even at this distance, Chi Wing hears its machinery needs oiling or readjustment. Sounds in the barracks wake him from dreams. Always, he is traveling. Moonlight filters through rolled-down black cloth curtains. The sound of the windmill is the rattle of his vehicle.

Every day, comrades use thick ropes and canvas belts to move boulders. Chi Wing works in a wide field, mounding earth around clusters of white melon seeds. He calls out to a boy from his barracks whose little red book is falling out of his pocket. The boy growls, and fear clutches Chi Wing. The boy is from Chengtu, a slum tough who hates Chi Wing's southern, educated voice. He pinches Chi Wing and would punch him if he would not be beaten by Lao Shen who hates everyone from the cities and sees no difference between beggars and bright boys. They are all counterrevolutionary, you can't get a good day's work out of any of them, and that's what's wrong with this country. Mao leads the way and only the peasants are strong enough to follow; the soft grabbers, readers, and measurers of air can't put fish head to melon mound worth a fart.

Chi Wing sees where Chengtu is looking, to the field where girls work. Chi Wing blushes; now he knows what Chengtu is doing. Lao Shen stamps about the melon mounds.

"Chairman Mao says we have enough bastards like you." Lao Shen enjoys the boys' lust and ogles the girls, too.

At red book meetings, they sit with girls in circles of eight with a leader who is older. Bump Girl has the biggest breasts that push out her blue jacket as if melons are inside. Needles always says, 'The point is....'

Tongueless never speaks, and the others Chi Wing knows are Giggler, Bad City Girl, and Flowerface, who receives real ribbons from Shanghai where someone is not afraid to buy 'capitalist-roading' gifts. All the boys have romantic fantasies about Flowerface, but they talk about getting into Bad City Girl. Her name is Lin; she also comes from Chengtu. Their leader often slaps Lin's face.

Planting near each other, Chi Wing means to help Lin. "All you do is mock. That does not build China."

"Fuck China and fuck you." Lin says she starts sex when Chi Wing starts 'measuring air'. "Put that little red book back in your pocket, take out what's bothering you and stick the rest of that shit in with the melon seeds."

Chi Wing is speechless.

"What're you staring at? Wha'd'ya think Mao's doing here? He's fucking without paying. At least I get coin for it in Chengtu!"

Chi Wing looks away to the windmill. "I can fix that."

"What else can you do?"

So begins a period of deceit Chi Wing realizes much later is the elementary school for his escape. He learns Lin's reverse-rules, her world of mirrors. When he lies in his bunk at night before he sneaks out to meet Lin, he remembers his sister playing the piano under a mirror in the common room at the university in Canton. He listens to Lin's plan to escape from the commune and agrees to improve it. She dreams of doing sex in Hong Kong, 'where Western coin buys the melons you stick in the mounds here'.

After they finish, he is soon ready but hesitates.

Lin reaches over in the dark and strokes his ear. Chi Wing thinks she likes him after all. Then the hardness of her voice hardens him more. "Any woman can take it ten times more than a man. The half of the sky Mao says we hold up? That's the heavy half."

They are taken on a trip to Peking, to Tiananmen Square. Chi Wing is overcome with nostalgia for city life. They parade by a re-viewing stand, part of the dark blue waves of China. At a signal, they are released and scatter. The immense square empties. Its hollowness fills him. When they return to Gansu, Lin is gone. She did it! In bed that night, he decides that when he escapes to leave directions behind for repairing the windmill. At first he does not believe he has courage to do it like Lin, but then word of his father's capitalist-roading sui-cide arrives, fixing the plan in Chi Wing's mind, an incantation of the three rivers he must cross: Yellow, Yangtze, Pearl. It takes Chi Wing two years to walk across China. Along the way, he loses his *pipa*, two teeth, and his few illusions about the New Order.

On a warm, misty October night in 1968, Chi Wing hides on a wooded hill within view of a small harbor of fishing boats. Here he cannot see the Nine Dragons of Kowloon, the mountains that shape the land to the south. His father's capitalist-roading spirit urges him forward. Behind him is the dark flow of the Yellow, Yangtze, Pearl.

In the water, there is only one thing to do: swim. He forgets to fear sharks. His arms reach a slimy piling. He smells tires, hears no voices. No *gogangu* teenage Gestapo on this side of the water! His chest aches, but he hauls himself onto the wooden dock. He awakens in a white-sheeted bed in the Holy Carpenter House in Hong Kong.

Three members of a panel from the National Cancer Institute are lunching at Chi Wing's apartment on Long Island, NY. The panel's senior member is Nobel winner Paul Whitney. The future of the Cold Spring Harbor Laboratory where Chi Wing does research relies upon the grant Whitney has the power to withhold or bestow. The men sit around a table cleared of grant application documents, now covered in a dark cloth. The task of entertaining the investigators belongs to Chi Wing as first assistant to the lab's chief, a woman Whitney despises.

"I've never met a woman with a first-rate mind. Why are your walls bare? I never saw bare walls in China."

Chi Wing brings tea things to the table. "Do you know *dazibao*?

"The wall posters, yes. I saw them in Peking in '79. I was taken to see them, as a matter of fact."

"You were there in a time oasis. My father's name is on *dazibao*."

Whitney understands. "I have only good memories of China; of the rock in the garden of Yu Yuan in Shanghai."

"T'ai-hu." Chi Wing imagines this notable Westerner officially posed by the great rock.

"My fondest memory is of climbing Tai Shan."

"I remember in Gansu, we raised melons no Chinese outside of Hong Kong tasted." Chi Wing pours tea. "Our field director was Lao Shen, an old man who had been given big white dentures by the 'barefoot doctors'. He wore those teeth only on formal occasions, but he carried them with him all the time. He said the girls' monthly curse withered the melons, but the girls joined in true communist fashion and their harvest dwarfed ours. He went crazy and the leaders became worried about his behavior when visitors came to our model commune. High party officials did come from Peking itself. Lao Shen roared into the meeting room and began screaming about women. He had a stroke and his teeth fell out of his pocket onto the table, chattering before the scandalized guests."

Like a magician, Chi Wing reaches into his chino slacks and pulls out fake false teeth with plastic gums, setting them on the table where they jump and rattle. The three startled guests recoil then explode with laughter.

Whitney stands and pockets the false teeth.

"What can be done about the grant proposal to improve its chances?" Chi Wing bows.

"That's easy. Have us rewrite it."

"That is too much to ask."

Whitney frowns and smiles at Chi Wing. "Is it?"

Chi Wing puts palms together. "It is an honor to see how it is done."

Oberon

To arrive at Northrop Frye's wedding ending of Comedy, villainies must be viewed askew.

For her daughter's second wedding anniversary in July, 2002, Hilde ordered a Wish List teapot of Meg's bridal pattern, Wedgwood Oberon, a modern revision of overwrought Jacobean vines. Also in July, 2002, though she had just retired, Hilde was astonished to be commissioned to rewrite the memoir of her husband's Aunt Florence, a Scottish octogenarian widow of a Japanese aristocrat. Florence's first husband had been a *zaibatsu*, educated in Japan, veneered at the University of Pennsylvania, Class of 1909, a champion who introduced golf to his native country and played with his neighbor, the young Emperor Hirohito. He was a close friend of Prime Minister Prince Fumimaro Konoe, the architect of the 1939 Nanking Massacre. This was a lot to take in and take on.

Florence, a Scottish nurse, resembled Carole Lombard in her movie magazine-like pictures, and her dapper husband, Baron Haruki 'Harry', didn't look his sixty-one to her twenty-five. Also included in the manuscript were other photos Florence had taken with a wedding gift camera from Baron Harry. These images of bridges and coves were confiscated by the wartime Japanese SS, the *kempetai*, and led to Florence's imprisonment which hawkish Tojo ordered to pressure the increasingly more doveish Prince Konoe.

How could Hilde refuse or resist rewriting the 1946 memoir? It had been revised in mid-1950s Manhattan, when a publisher assigned a then-unknown editor – Betty Friedan – to work with Brian's Aunt Florence. Friedan's 'Cinderella story' version had outraged its author, who shelved the book for decades. In 1963 NYC, when Hilde was sixteen and first met Brian's aunt, she was warned never to ask Florence about what had happened in Japan.

In 1996, Hilde's play about her Wellesley 1969's twenty-fifth month-before-the-first-Moon-landing class' *Lunar Reunion* won awards and nationwide productions. Her classmate, First Lady Hillary Clinton, saw it in Washington DC and sent a note that Hilde guessed a secretary had penned. She doubted her classmate remembered her at all. "We went to different Wellesleys," Hilde always said when asked, "even though our names were often confused. She was Hillary Rodham, and I was Hil-de – 'Hill-dee' – Rodman. Professors saw the name on their roster, and then I appeared in class and their hearts sank. I was not The Hill, just Hill-D. I had an English professor, a lesbian Icelandic scholar who looked like Popeye's Olive Oil, who called me 'Hill-D-alloway' for good measure."

By February, 2003, Hilde had researched and rewritten Florence's memoir. She told friends that it was like getting another Master's degree, this time in modern Japanese history. Florence approved it, and Hilde placed it with her agent. Then as suddenly as can be said of someone who was eighty-eight, Aunt Florence died. In her will, she left Hilde the manuscript. In May a year later, an obituary in the *New York Times* for Japan's hundred and one year old first post-war representative at the UN stopped Hilde cold. Florence's Baron Harry had been chosen before this man, but he'd died of a heart attack at the very party given to celebrate his UN appointment. Hilde contacted a *Times* reporter who'd interviewed the centenarian's heir, an internationally known rightwing journalist and longtime associate of then-campaigning VP Cheney. Through the *Times* reporter, Hilde contacted Hajime – 'Jimmy' – who invited her to send him Florence's memoir.

As he read the attachment Hilde emailed, he wrote nostalgic replies about childhood memories of the history he had in common with Florence and Baron Harry, more often ridiculing her descriptions of people and events. He offered to recommend the memoir to his friend the emeritus Kodansha publisher – if Hilde would make Jimmy's rightwing edits and hand deliver the manuscript hard copy to him during his next trip to DC 'in November and drink champagne' at the GOP celebration he anticipated after the 2004 re-election. Dick Cheney and Don Rumsfeld, Jimmy wrote, were, like the man at Kodansha, old friends. Her agent was encouraging.

An email *pas de deux* ensued. With polite verbal sidesteps following the emailed advice of the Asian Studies Chair at Harvard, whom she had contacted during research, Hilde demurred the edits she knew would have been anathema to Florence. She added her own excuses for her absence at the command performance: in November, she was moving from NYC to Rhode Island because Meg was in mid-residency and pregnant, due in March.

Jimmy just as diplomatically admired her *entrechat*. He praised Hilde's play *Lunar Reunion*, wondering if 'it owed its four-plot structure to *Midsummer Night's Dream*?' and sent her several translated editions of his eighty-five books, including the one that denied the Peking Massacre. He reinvited Hilde to dance for the devil in May. How could she not hear echoes of Oberon? *When I had at my pleasure taunted her, And she in mild terms begg'd my patience, I then did ask of her her changeling child...*

Folding space, as in branes/brains, increases information storage and demonstrates that topology equals geography.

The world truly reiterated Mandelbrot's fractals. After more than three decades as an editor, in retirement after 2002, Hilde had the time to learn how many names the same objects could have. On a Sunday in May, 2005, the Northeast Regional from Boston to DC stopped for passengers where the aboriginal 'rocky river' Sneechte-connet-then-Blackstone changed its name to the Providence River as it flowed into the Atlantic-called-the-Sound between Connecticut and Long Island. Hilde and Brian weren't required to change trains at Penn Station in New York. Awaiting departures/arrivals, they sat fifty feet beneath the paradoxically horizontal body of the vertical city, familiar and missed, lying above her like a lost love, Leonardo's Vitruvian Man. She knew the weight of the city intimately, its borough-border finger-tips and feet, its Manhattan lungs and lights. It felt personal when the train pulled out.

After seven hours from Providence to DC, along with other mistaken travelers, Hilde and Brian nearly disembarked at the penultimate station when the conductor called out 'Washington, DC,' but it was a stop for locals who quickly directed them back onto the train.

There was no mistaking the last stop at Union Station, from which they could walk to their small hotel. Trees were in full green leaf, and the air warm summer to Rhode Island's cool spring. The hotel was better than expected; they were led to a tiny duplex, bedroom and bath upstairs, half bath and sitting room below. In the time before they were expected at dinner on Connecticut Avenue, Brian poured Hilde single malt from a flask, and she tried to calm down.

A cab took them to an Indian restaurant in Cleveland Park. A round table was set for nine, four couples and their Japanese host. Brian was seated with the wives of the Cheney/Rumsfeld men from the DOD, and Jimmy nodded to the solicitous maitre d' to pull out the chair beside him for Hilde. Three shots of Glenfiddich back in the hotel room had fortified Hilde sufficiently to feel more observant than observed. Jimmy looked younger than his late seventies, his face as smooth as his manner. He was shorter than Brian, and thicker, with a squared head and jaw. He wore a dark suit and blue shirt and smelled of bergamot, like Earl Grey tea. Hilde remembered a phrase she had once questioned in an edit, 'a five hundred dollar tie,' possibly verified by the navy paisley worn by her host. Clearly but curiously, Jimmy had invited her to be his guest of honor at the table on this Sunday evening.

The three DOD men and their tired wives looked like they were as on order as the food. The tallest and oldest of the men had wavy white hair and a deep Southern accent. Hilde figured he saluted Cheney/Rumsfeld, the other two obviously subordinates. Jimmy leaned in and whispered to Hilde, "The Vice President would have joined us but—" and waved away the rest of his insincerity. Drinks came several times before dinner. Hilde, rarely more than a one drink pony, could not feel her teeth, but the alcohol had done little to quiet the echoes of Florence's undiminished fears and warnings never to contact anyone in Japan.

Jimmy was asking her about the food, and then abruptly said, "Are you a Christian?"

Hilde retasted the maraschino in her Old Fashioned. Words from *Macbeth* sped across her mental news-crawl: *'Have we eaten on the insane root that takes the reason prisoner?'* Message received, Brain.

Ask, never answer questions. It can't end badly, can it? Smile.

"What would Jesus say?"

"You were a classmate of the former First Lady."

"We went to different Wellesleys."

"How so?"

"Do you think birth order might play a role? Hillary is an older sister, and I'm a younger one."

"Who would think you were even the same age?"

Hilde felt defensive, though not for herself. Jimmy's diplomacy was as fine as forty percent of the paintings – forgeries – hanging in the world's greatest museums. Focus. Hillary. Then Hilde heard herself reading aloud from her news-crawl: "*Some are born great, some achieve greatness, and some have greatness thrust upon them* – oh, that's Malvolio, reading from the fraudulent letter." So maybe she was drunk, but it was the truth. She added, "Hillary is the trifecta," and looked across the table at Brian. He was listening to one of the wives, a forty-something woman wearing a pitiful green suit. She was worrying about her children, and her husband was alternately disapproving of or ignoring her. Brian said something kind, and the woman's eyes softened. Then the man to Hilde's left began describing the War College where he was on the part-time faculty. His accent was less pronounced but also Southern. Jimmy easily interrupted him and refilled her wine glass.

"Tell me about Wellesley."

Hilde remembered aggressive Harvard boys; she had learned

bullies only respected a bigger bully. A facial expression poised between promise and derision worked best.

"Because the campuses are so beautiful, people used to say that God would send a son to Princeton and a daughter to Wellesley."

"Like Eden."

"Without the temptation of boys and snakes."

Jimmy laughed, echoed by the DOD. Hilde thought: there used to be smoke-filled rooms where men like these moved in clouds of power and paid courtesans to punish their sins with pleasure. The twenty-first century outlawed smoking and democratized power.

"At our graduation, Hillary was the first student ever to be the invited speaker at a Wellesley Commencement. We cheered when she used the word 'ecstatic' in front of—" but Jimmy stopped her.

Leaning in again, he said, "Bring the memoir to breakfast tomorrow at my hotel at ten a.m."

"I have it here, now. The maitre d' has—"

But with the same wave, Jimmy dismissed her words and gestured a waiter over for dessert orders which only Hilde and Brian declined.

Regarding the demolition and reconstruction of great buildings, architects must think about both aesthetics and mechanics.

Facing the White House across Lafayette Square, The Hay-Adams was a boutique hotel rebuilt above the razed mansions of Henry Adams and John Hay, personal secretary to President Abraham Lincoln, and later U.S. Ambassador to the United Kingdom, as well as

Secretary of State under both William McKinley and Theodore Roosevelt. Together with their wives, Clara Hay and Clover Adams, as well as noted geologist Clarence King, Hay and Adams formed a group they named the 'Five of Hearts' and had custom china made in that pattern.

Hilde didn't ask at the desk for a taxi to the Hay-Adams. She walked outside on the warm May morning and was approached by a black man in livery offering her his limousine.

"That's some fancy car," she hesitated.

"You're some fancy lady," he replied.

She accepted being gulled. On the quick trip to Lafayette Square, the chauffeur continued charming her with anecdotes about the government buildings they passed. Hilde watched suited men and women entering and exiting, and thought DC looked like where, minus green apples, Magritte's bowler hats must land. She gripped the cardboard box with Florence's memoir on her lap.

Jimmy was not in the hotel lobby when she walked in. She looked around at the ornate wood and marble; Clover Adams had never lived here. Hilde was directed up a short flight of steps to a brilliant, nearly empty dining room made as glaring as a field of snow by tables covered in layered white linens. A waiter, also in a white jacket, led her to a table farthest from the tall, bright windows. Jimmy stood to welcome her and took the manuscript out of her hands, placing it out of sight on one of the four chairs at the table.

They sat. She wondered if his suite was on the fourth floor where the ghost of Clover Adams was said to walk early in the winter month when she had committed suicide in 1885. *Gothic mood. Snap out of it.* Hilde focused on the flowers and formal table setting – fragrant, pale pink peonies quite possibly harboring ants, butter plates, cups and saucers. Another waiter appeared with a tray carrying both a coffee and a teapot.

"I know this pattern. It's my daughter's wedding china – Wedgwood Oberon."

Context returned. She could see Meg's face and the baby. She calmed. This stranger was not the Japanese sandman of her grandmother's lullaby. Jimmy had real plans for his current DC trip lobbying for rightwing Japanese interests, for which she had been – a convenience, an *amuse bouche* at a dinner. She was not among the more than two birds to get with one stone. She was hardly even a pebble under which Jimmy might find some dirt on Hillary that could oil future encounters with Cheney/Rumsfeld. Eagles did not fly with chicka-or-Hil-dees. Why had he insisted on this morning meeting? It was no more than that a man does not live by breakfast alone.

"Wedgwood," Jimmy lifted his cup. "English china. Charles Darwin was Wedgwood's grandson. He married his first cousin, who was also a Wedgwood grandchild. My first cousin is Yoko Ono."

Hilde had intended complimenting the strong jasmine tea she was sipping. Instead she blurted, "You must love springing that on people!"

Jimmy basked. "Why, do you think I am so different from my

cousin?"

"Yoko Ono! You two are like – migratory birds! Eighteen hundred of the world's ten thousand bird species are migratory. Like me, the rest are called resident or sedentary."

"Oh, we are more rare than eighteen per cent."

"Your Thanksgiving table conversation must be epic. Florence wrote nothing about Thanksgiving in Japan, perhaps because as a Scot she would not have missed it."

"We do have a November harvest festival, Labor Thanksgiving Day. *Kinro Kansha no Hi* is actually a modern name for an ancient ritual called *Niinamesai*, our harvest festival. In the ritual, the Emperor makes the season's first offering of freshly harvested rice to the gods and then partakes of the rice himself."

At which apparent cue, a waiter wheeled a silver tray of breakfast foods and served them.

Splitting open a steaming scone for which she had no appetite, Hilde said, "Has your trip to DC been—"

"...Lengthy," Jimmy interrupted as he continued to concentrate on raspberries and sliced green gage plums. "There is too much piracy in the East China Sea and an ongoing dispute about our Senkaku Islands."

"...Which the Chinese call *Diaoyu*."

"I am surprised you follow this." Jimmy refilled his cup with coffee, then hers with tea.

"Florence's memoir opens Western eyes on Japan. From the

moment in Shanghai in 1939, when she was a young nurse from Scotland and *'the military tanks rumbled into the main courtyard of the country hospital only that morning, in the wake of General Wu, who now lies safely tucked in bed.'"*

"The Chinese have a different view of history. Did you know the invading American Army looted and raped? That is not reported in your history books."

"In China?"

"In Japan."

"General MacArthur," Hilde added, "ordered all such indefensible atrocities reported directly to him. As your cousin's full page *Times* ads repeatedly proclaim, unnecessary war is the worst crime."

"Necessity is the mother of dissension. At Wellesley, did you resent Mrs. Clinton?"

"Oh, she'll always be Ms. Rodham to me. Truly, about Hillary, there are no Shakespearian lean and hungry looks from the likes of me. I identify with Pindarus' escapist politics. 'Far from this country Pindarus shall run, where never Roman shall take note of him. Or her.'"

"That is impossible for any Roman Senator."

"Yes, it is also good not to be king," Hilde agreed. "Lear shouldn't have divested. Hamlet cursed having to set things right."

"Why do you pursue the memoir? You were not born, she was not your aunt, and now she is dead."

"Well, if mortality is thesis, memory is antithesis. Synthesis? Her

Scottish brogue was music."

"Bagpipes?"

"No, Florence's voice was lovely, like Cordelia's. She had no idea Baron Harry was *zaibatsu*. She worried he could lose his job for marrying her, a non-Japanese, so she assured him she would work to support them as a nurse. In that teahouse in Tokyo, in moonlight, he took both her hands and didn't laugh. He had tears in his eyes when he said, 'Oh, my dear, you will never need to fear that.' I think he married Florence because she was the incarnation of an Impressionist portrait he'd bought in the nineteen twenties from the Louvre – I never could track it down. That painting was incinerated along with Baron Harry's house and much of Tokyo in a May 1945 raid, two months after the Operation Meeting-house firebombing, worse than either Hiroshima or Nagasaki in August. I also never found the woman doctor who'd returned from Germany after creating diets for Holocaust survivors, who saved Florence's life when she got to LA in 1946."

"Have you seen her ghost?"

Hilde now recognized his abrupt pattern, but this veered steeply. Suddenly, he was unnerved and unnerving.

"Here?' Hilde stalled. "Clover Adams only comes in early December. She hugs people and whispers 'what do you want?' I once edited an article about wet macular degeneration. It affects sight. Hallucination is an entirely sane symptom."

His black eyes were focusing beyond Hilde, and his lips moved silently. Then he flattened his palms on the white tablecloth table. "My flight is at three p.m. So…"

Hilde moved the manuscript onto the table. As if conjured, another apparition of white-jacketed waiter stood behind her ready to draw back her chair. Jimmy's dismissal made her giddy with relief. She nodded to the waiter, indicating the boxed memoir, and the young man assented, as if any of it mattered. Only four per cent of the porous universe was what we and our dreams were made of.

No two events which are simultaneous with reference to the railway embankment are not also simultaneous relatively to the train.

The Acela from DC to Boston was an express. As they sped north, greenery diminished in density and color saturation, and it looked like they were traveling back in time from summer to spring.

"What?" Brian woke her.

"What?"

"You were talking in your sleep."

"What was I saying?"

Brian folded the *Times* onto his lap. "You were saying no to Einstein, then Potsdam, Bloom, Professor Harold, I'm guessing, and you were smiling. Maybe you caught Jimmy's crazy."

Hilde was half asleep. "I saw Aunt Florence standing in her living room, August, 1945, so hot and hungry in Japan, when Konoe secretly brought the Potsdam Declaration to read aloud to her to see if he understood every English nuance and his tiny aide who wrote later, disapproving of her short-shorts." Her eyes opened. She was awake. "But it's gone now – Einstein said no. What about?"

"God doesn't play dice with the universe?"

"Not that one. Something else."

"Or you dreamed it."

"But you saw the email: Bloom said I was right, Shakespeare imagined everything – but the future."

"What do you think Aunt Florence's memoir's chances are now?"

"Better, if she's haunting him. If he even took it back to Japan with him – dubious at best; a man with many ghosts, mad as the Hatter."

"It was hardly a trip to Wonderland, Alice."

"At least we kept our heads."

When the train approached New York, it took a long, banking curve on unfamiliar tracks. Sunset gilded a tilted skyline against massing purple rainclouds. On her return, the city looked like a stranger to Hilde. As on their honeymoon decades before, Brian slept beside her when the train picked up speed. It became a dark and stormy night punctuated by lightning and thunder. Waves of rain gusted against black, mirroring windows. Along the Connecticut shore, Hilde couldn't see the Sound beside the tracks or over brief bridges when the train was suspended above water. All she could see was her reflection as the Acela slowed and came to their stop in Providence.

Triptych

"...while my glory passes by I will put you in a cleft of the rock, and I will cover you with my hand until I have passed by. Then I will take away my hand, and you shall see my back, but my face shall not be seen." Exodus 33:22-23

Even when you grow up in Manhattan, everything you know is self-absorbed, *unum*; the *pluribus* comes much later. Phyllis grew up imagining that she could shape-shift like Alice in Wonderland. At the Metropolitan Museum of Art on Fifth Avenue, she could grow small and climb the ivory stairs inside carved medieval miniatures. Near the dinosaurs at the Museum of Natural History, Phyllis imagined she loomed large.

Born in 1968, she had been a privileged only child. At forty, she was employed at the Museum as a restorer. As an intern through her father's art world connections, she had known John Brealey before his stroke in 1989, head of the Paintings Conservation Department and one of the most important practitioners of the twentieth century. Phyllis had been divorced for ten years. When she turned forty, both her parents had died, her mother from leukemia. Her father, a syndicated cartoonist, had been backed into by a car mistakenly thrown into reverse by a tourist overwhelmed by Manhattan traffic.

A front page *New York Times* photo showed Phyllis at work on a triumph, the restoration of a late nineteenth century family portrait of a Belle Epoque President of the New York Stock Exchange. For its image of burgher status, it invoked comparison to Rembrandt's *Night Watch*. When rediscovered in storage in the Met, the giant painting had been in pieces. It had been lost since the 1929 stock market crash destroyed the Matchby family's fortune. The *Times* photo showed Phyllis in a white coat with her auburn hair in a bun. Her raised right arm, poised with tool, cast a large shadow on the canvas. On a table in the foreground lay open blueprint-like pages. Referring to this *grimoire*, Phyllis looked like a necromancer conjuring forth the proud upper class family as her thin brush daubed clean their red velvet drapes. Phyllis and her team had solved problems of relining, cleansing, in-painting and filling the huge canvas, bringing it back from the shadows to the light of current day.

Phyllis owned a one bedroom apartment in a 60's building near the UN. She had a grand piano instead of a table in her dining alcove and a plasma TV on the wall of the bedroom. Her divorce and parents' deaths had numbed Phyllis. The painting assigned to her team was the quintessential piece for a major autumn exhibit. When Phyllis had seen the jigsaw pieces of the Matchby on a tarp spread on a basement floor, she felt something. Her team insisted that a daughter in the portrait looked just like Phyllis.

The Matchby family portrait presented fifteen people: grandparents, the stock exchange president and his wife, their eleven children, and a pet monkey on the lap of the sister who was Phyllis' avatar. Restoration work on the monkey activated some hormone dormant in Phyllis until then and inversely proportional to its previous absence.

Jian Dolan had been trying to get Phyllis' attention. He'd discovered that they lived two floors apart. She was attractive and single, but it had been obvious to him that she couldn't see him for dirt, or possibly for his unshaven beard. His Chinese maternal *waipo* in Shanghai disdained this hirsute genetic inheritance from Jian's Irish-American father. Both his parents had died, which for Jian always cued Lady Bracknell in Oscar Wilde's *The Importance of Being Earnest*: 'To lose one parent, Mr. Worthing, may be regarded as a misfortune; to lose both looks like carelessness.' He was a Chinese translator at the UN. The pay wasn't baronial, especially by NYC standards, but... he warned people to take a breath... his wife had died in one of the Towers, so he'd inherited enough to buy the apartment in Phyllis' building and live on a federal salary.

Jian shaved his beard; Phyllis noticed him on the elevator. He had the face of the younger boy on the red loveseat in the Matchby portrait! *Coup de foudre*!

Phyllis and Jian were sharing the elevator with a man a decade younger who was getting home from work and still working. The silk tie loosened at his throat was the only concession he'd made to his physical absence from whatever office. He was multi-tasking on his BlackBerry, texting and talking, likely buying and selling at the same time. He got off a floor before Phyllis.

In the interim she commented, "Ozymandias."

Jian took the cue, reciting, "Look on my works, ye Mighty, and despair," and asked her out to a late dinner. In the restaurant, he tried trivia-masked erudition. "Ozymandias represents a transliteration into Greek of a pharaoh's name, *User-maat-re Setep-en-re*."

Phyllis showed Jian the museum shop's gold ring that replaced her wedding band. The hieroglyph for the Queen of Heaven was stamped in black enamel. "Shelley's poem describes Pharaoh Rameses II. He sired more children than any other Egyptian king."

"There were a lot of kids in the Matchby portrait."

"Did you go to see it?"

"Yes," he admitted. "I saw you in the *Times* photo."

Already burning, Phyllis melted. "You look just like one of the sons in the painting."

By the next morning, both late for work, they were a couple.

Good fortune followed: an April wedding and honeymoon in Shanghai, and an elderly neighbor died. A year after the autumn Matchby exhibit, Phyllis and Jian moved into the larger condo on a higher floor. When they learned they were expecting a baby in May, they celebrated like tourists and ascended to the one hundred and second floor observatory deck of the Empire State Building. Cold October gusts hit the glass enclosure and the light was so glaring, they had to turn their backs away from it, like Moses shielded in the cleft of rock.

Baby showers filled the nursery with merchandise that accompanied items sent from Jian's relatives in China. In the delivery room, neither Phyllis nor Jian noticed the look between nurse and obstetrician. The infant required a feeding tube. Genetic testing began. Chromosomes that Jian lacked, Phyllis had not compensated. A familiar numbness enveloped Phyllis.

Jian found himself thrown backward in time to the horror and guilt of 9/11. On her normal commute uptown, his wife Janice had seen she had his phone along with her own, so she reversed trains and rushed to the Trade Center to get it to him before he would begin translating for a CEO at a Windows on the World breakfast meeting. On that cloudless September day, Jian had dawdled walking to and from the subway. Then he saw, exploding high above him, pillars of black smoke and fire. Ignorant that Janice was in an elevator arriving at the intersection of history, Jian ran to escape the volcanic billows racing north on Vesey. He came to, whitened like a George Segal statue, on the other side of the Brooklyn Bridge, when he realized his phone was missing and he couldn't call Janice to reassure her. Ironies vied with tragedies like crossing riptides in the ensuing days.

2

Human history is a chronicle of miscommunication with the Divine which no more understands us than we do It. Jian Dolan

For eight weeks until she could survive without a feeding tube, Lily Minfong was kept in the hospital NICU. Jian tried to explain to his grandmother in Shanghai about 'Lilmin'. His *waipo* kept repeating *canfei* or *canji*, and Jian became speechless. He couldn't translate how he and Phyllis were being trained with saline on gelled manikin forearms to begin at three months injecting the baby nightly. He could not tell his *waipo* that when they brought Lilmin home, they slept sexlessly with the infant beside them in her co-sleeper nor that life was a contest between entropy and conservation of matter and energy.

Four days a week, a day nurse took care of the baby, and on the other three Jian and Phyllis rotated work schedules. There were weekly bouts of physical therapy. Alone with Lilmin in the apartment, Jian began to hear conversations through the walls. He heard similar voices at work, speaking a foreign language. He began to recognize rhythms, then meaning. As August ended, Jian felt anxious when he couldn't hear the voices. Only the fatherly voice that called itself The Director calmed him.

The letter Jian left behind at The Director's order explained, apologized, and legally documented his mental incompetence. Jian had gone looking for *hailuoyin* in Chinatown and found *ma fei*. After Phyllis left for the museum on September eleventh, Jian filled a syringe with morphine rather than growth hormone. The Director soothed Jian. 'Lilmin will never scream again.' She rested in peace in her stroller beside him in the park over-looking the East River when Jian administered his own fatal dose. The Director intended Phyllis to 'share the city's anniversary condolences'. Jian closed the dictated letter with his own paraphrased translation of Saramago's *CAIN* about the building of the Tower of Babel. The life insurance company lacked grounds for contest; Phyllis collected as well as inherited.

3

'What are those of the known, but to ascend and enter the Unknown? And what are those of life, but for Death?' Whitman, *Portals*.

A decade later, Phyllis dawdled getting to work on a warm September Friday morning, arriving at the Met's fifth floor Conservation Center with its large easels and skylights. She had picked up bouquets of sunflowers from a Korean stand. Already at work, two interns were at work on a previously unknown Toeput Tower of Babel, the second half of a 1587 diptych. The second Toeput Babel had recently surfaced in a Norwegian museum out of the inexhaustible Goering trove of loot on the Art Loss Register. The Toeput's provenance had been verified by the daughter of the deceased owner, who lived on the West Side in the same apartment her father had purchased, along with his exit from 1938 Germany, with the money from its sale.

Most Babels depicted the construction of the Tower, but like the known Toeput, this new one showed a photographic next frame of impending destruction. It depicted the macula-bird shadow overtaking the unfinished building's conical apex, but the Tower was farther in the background. The painting focused instead on people in the foreground: interrupted workers, horrified onlookers, people fleeing, or some, as Auden described in his poem of Icarus' fall, utterly indifferent to catastrophe.

Phyllis' entrance quieted the workroom, except for 'Afro-Aaron', her first assistant, who took the bouquets from her hand and waved a ticket he pulled out of his shirt pocket.

"Here you are. I've had these two tickets to…" He named the most sought-after Broadway show. "…for months, but I received a better offer." He smiled at an intern who, Phyllis noted, blushed metameric shades of crimson.

"I'm leaving the other one at the box office for my college classmate…" Aaron repeated the TV star's bio. "After escaping Mo-les-Station, Texas, for good, from the start of his freshman year at Cooper Union in New York, Marshall Bekins appeared in soaps, and by graduation had appeared in three feature films. At thirty-six, he co-stars in a TV series—"

"—that shoots in New York, now in its fourth season," the interns recited.

At eight that evening, she found herself seated beside the actor who had tried to enter undetected as the theater darkened, but like iron filings the audience swayed magnetically around him. He took the aisle seat and offered his hand. Aaron had introduced her in absentia. Before the intermission, they laughed at the same line of dialogue; 'I'm a lapsed existentialist.'

Marshall invited Phyllis for a drink. The maitre d' obviously had a crush on the actor, and they were immediately well-seated in the crowded restaurant. Wait staff hovered around their booth, moths near flame. Phyllis translated the look in his uncanny blue eyes to mean that he shared her desire for closed doors.

"Let's get out of here," Marshall said. "I live two blocks away."

His apartment was dark. The walls were white and bare. There were few lamps to turn on. He lighted two joints at once then put one in her mouth.

"'Now, Voyager...'" Phyllis quoted.

"'...Sail thou forth, to seek and find.'" The actor imitated Claude Rains. "Doctor Jaquith tells her to read the Whitman. Usually you'll hear a Bette Davis impression," he said. "'Oh, Jerry, don't let's ask for the moon. We have the stars!'"

"What perfect mimicry! Are you bi—?"

"—Lingual? —Lateral? A straight line is a tangent to a curve."

"There's no calculus to life." Phyllis coughed. "I haven't inhaled since college."

Marshall blew a backspin smoke ring and sat down. "Odd name: Toeput. Aaron talked about your restoration."

Phyllis sat facing him, dazed by the marijuana. "It gets odder. Otter," she nearly giggled. "Lodewijk Toeput, il Pozzoserrato, was a sixteenth century mannerist landscape painter from Antwerp who spent most of his life in Italy. Pozzoserrato means closed well."

"Like Pozzo in *Godot*?"

Phyllis kept rambling. "Master Brealey insisted that the skills associated with restorers were 'not nearly enough to bring to the business, which is really the life and death of paintings. Colored muds held together by a sticky substance – that's painting.' One of the rules of modern restoration is that everything done must be able to be undone."

Marshall exhaled spiced smoke. "I don't follow you." He stood, again offering his hand. He seemed as tall as a tower above her.

"Then I'll follow you."

Marshall's night doorman had bet himself that he would get the woman a cab before dawn; he considered Phyllis' generous tip his winnings. She had intended to leave earlier, but Marshall had awakened when she went to the bathroom. Astride by city light through the blinds, she had seen the actor's beautiful face relax from orgasm into a deep sleep he would awaken from before noon, feeling inexplicably rejected.

The next time Aaron and Marshall saw each other was in late November, at a Village restaurant for the annual Un-Family Thanksgiving they had created as undergrads. They had not had spoken to each other since September. Marshall's persistence had pressed Phyllis at one point to beg for Aaron's intercession, but he was caught up in his own unfortunate fall: like the original Adam, the blushing intern had left in disgrace after a questionable theft. Aaron knew Marshall would never ask about Phyllis, but the answer was visible in the foreground of the Babel restoration. There, Toeput had painted Aaron's African face, and the two figures shouldering burdens were recognizably Phyllis running from Marshall, resisting the irresistible.

Time and Tide

"If you set a story in 1320 Europe, you've got to know that in twenty-eight years, bubonic plague will cross the Channel and continue annihilating half your unsuspecting characters. If you set a story in the present day, you know you're equally blind to an inevitable future."

Not that Marjorie's husband, Byrd, a newly-minted Reiki Master in Manhattan, visibly reacted to his wife's remark as he passed by her associates in the living room en route to the renovated kitchen, but he did stop – pause – in his mind. In the past several years, Marjorie's hobby/obsession – writing historical novels – had miraculously paid off. One of the first three had won a national award, but the one about Bach's second wife, Anna Magdalena, had taken off, become a bestseller in the genre, been optioned for a movie, and resulted in new representation and contracts for at least two more novels. In the business, she had progressed from having a nice deal, onto a good deal, and was hopefully headed toward significant and major ones. Whatever labels attached to higher eyries were beyond Byrd's flights of imagination. All this, as bookstores and publishers shuddered and toppled like Middle Eastern dictatorships, both fundamentally supplanted by novel –Byrd punned – technologies.

Byrd's passage to the kitchen had been no idle journey; it was intended to cue Marjorie to end the authors' club morning meeting so their trip to the ocean could commence. After three feet of snow and bitter temperatures that winter, the January thaw had finally arrived for Valentine's Day week, all the more to be celebrated. They were expected in Freeport on Long Island. Nevertheless, in the kitchen Byrd toyed with the new stainless espresso maker and poured a foamy fragrant cup that he sipped at on his return to the study – the small second bedroom in this upper West side building where Marjorie had lived all her life, inherited from her parents. Rent-controlled in the West eighties, now renovated by her royalties, the apartment was the steal of the still-young century. Byrd's earlier moment of inner cessation had filled with wonder: how had this son of the south found himself in this place and time after all – and what was to follow, what was following/awaiting him in the blind future?

In the south, Byrd had grown morbidly obese, and his first wife and now adult children had looked to him like marionettes he'd seen at a country club wedding, cavorting to the melody and lyrics of *Dixie*. Byrd had met Marjorie after he'd written a fan letter via her first publisher. He had explained that as a principal in an advertising/marketing firm in Mississippi, he'd Googled through Baroque music to Bach's *Joy of Man's Desiring* for one purpose and located instead Marjorie's novel about Anna Magdalena Bach. Then he'd felt a compulsion to read her book and – 'perhaps Bach's *Sleepers, awake!* would have been the more apt title for me.' His forwarded letter had a similar effect on Marjorie, who had snailed him a hand-written reply along with his requested/reimbursed autographed copy of *Joy*. Thereafter, their courtly correspondence rivaled Cyrano's and Roxane's, lacking only the Bergerac nose and duplicity.

Byrd left his wife and Mississippi. He married Marjorie, and on her health insurance because he was unemployed in Manhattan, he had bariatric surgery, the complications from which resulted in a successful malpractice suit that underwrote his Reiki education and certification. Three hundred pounds lighter, as if released from a prison of flesh, Byrd found acolytes, clients, and a decent cash flow. Marjorie's books sold lucratively: she retired from her research job of three decades, located in a sliver of a building designed by Stanford White near the Empire State.

Once the society of historical fiction authors would leave their living room, Byrd and Marjorie would walk through the warm oasis of February sunshine to the subway to Penn Station, and from there descend to the Long Island Railroad train, rising to Freeport, to Guy Lombardo Avenue, to the Nautical Mile, to a restaurant overlooking an inlet of the Atlantic where gambling cruise ships slowly moved into tax-free waters. The black couple they would meet in Freeport for lunch would take them afterwards to Point Lookout. Offsummer season, there, they could walk freely along the beach by the jetties and the waves. They had socialized with the Thornes several times before, in the city and on the Island, after Ernelle had introduced herself as a fan much as Byrd had. Ernelle Thorne was a high school music teacher. Her husband Charles, a doctor, ribbed Byrd about Reiki in an easy-going way.

"So Rei energy had a frequency of seventy-two hundred cps? That the same as hertz?"

"I'm sure I don't know."

"That's a twenty-five mile long wave." Charles spread his arms. "That's some long wave, moving at the speed of light, cycling every one seventy-two hundredth of a second. It boggles the mind. How do you get your hands on that?

"Let me know when you've done the math."

The men socialized with the mutual indifference of book covers to their wives' aligned interior pages. How apt the démodé bookbinding metaphor was for the sexagenarians, Byrd thought, in this age of e-books where Marjorie's novels also sold well. Befriending the black Thornes was just another piece of the new jigsaw puzzle of Byrd's northern life. This brave new world was new to him.

It was extraordinary how it was the same sky and atmosphere over the city, but beside the ocean, the air and light were altogether different. The ground underfoot, neither asphalt nor cement, was sand, in dunes, on lips, alive with puckers of hidden clams. Near a splashed jetty lay a flat Germanic helmet molted by a horseshoe crab. It attracted and appalled Marjorie. 'A prehistoric hieroglyph,' she called it, running away towards the next jetty, each one marking the beach like a musical staff. There were only a few notes – people – on the beach on a February Wednesday afternoon.

At first, the women walked together and the men followed. Byrd walked to the rhythm of the waves, but Doctor Thorne slowed, examining the seascape.

"The tide's rising," he observed. "Humans are 'ugly bags of mostly water.' … about sixty percent. Y'know, you see plenty of unexplained phenomena in medicine."

Byrd felt a pulse of connection. "*Star Trek, Next Generation. Home Soil*. Great episode."

Doctor Thorne continued in the same reflective tone. "But 'for example' is never proof." With a friendly nod, he walked ahead to catch up with the women.

Byrd contentedly returned to the ocean's beat. He enjoyed watching Marjorie fluttering on land while terns and gulls flew over the water, clusters of them alighting like one thought on a wave, jetty, or now-unchaired lifeguard mound. Byrd had grown up beside – out of, he sometimes fantasized – the great river that smelled of stones, mud, and catfish. He could smell the Mississippi in his mind, contrasting it to the salty Atlantic. Like a comma, a premier moon crescent punctuated the afternoon sky. Byrd sighed. 'In equal scale weighing delight and dole,' he was sorry and smug to invoke

Claudius. He saw ahead of him Marjorie and their acquaintances stopped at the water's edge, blocking his view of whatever had halted their progress. As he closed the distance, he saw a big man, bald and clothed in flannel shirt and ankle-soaked jeans, barefoot, sweating with his nearly finished labor. Byrd put his left arm around the waist of Marjorie's thick leather jacket. He could feel her disturbed *byosen*. She reached up to cover his mouth with her hand, to keep him silent.

Before them was a sand sculpture of a giant octopus so realistic it caused an instinctive recoil, its back to the ocean, facing inland. Its suckered arms were positioned to appear partially underwater – the sand – and partially dragging under its prey whose shoulders and head clearly identified it as the sculptor himself. The entire sculpture – octopus & artist – was just as clearly immediate prey of the rising tide. Each new breaking wave brought sea foam closer to drowning the tableau and dispatching its creator.

Byrd felt Marjorie trembling against him; her aura was the palest green. How easily she was given to episodes of overwhelmed intensity. She could concentrate herself into another time and place so completely that she would speak in whatever foreign language she was researching. She often reacted to awakening from a dream as if kidnapped like Oliver Twist. Now she twisted against Byrd's embrace.

"*Just for today, just for today.*" Byrd chanted the mantra and moved his right hand clockwise against her back, behind her pounding heart. He felt his palms transferring healing energy. He breathed in light and breathed it out, "*Anahata*," into Marjorie's fourth chakra.

The sculptor put finishing touches on the octopus. A wave splashed the artist, and this time the cold water made him shiver and run up the beach, close to Byrd and the others. The black couple had taken out their cell phones and were about to take and send photos.

"Stop!" the sculptor barked. "No!"

Marjorie's eyes filled. She moved beyond Byrd's calming touch, shaking her head at the Thornes. "No," she echoed, more gently, reassuring the chagrined couple.

After they left Point Lookout, they drove to Long Beach and walked on the boardwalk. There were young mothers with strollers, one or two retirees on bicycles, and some blank-eyed elderly lined up in sweaters and jackets behind glass in the King David old age home.

"In 1914," Marjorie tour-guided, "elephants from Coney Island's Dreamland were brought here to help haul pilings to build the board-walk, but it was a publicity stunt by a man named Reynolds, the Donald Trump of the time. Verne and Irene Castle – you know the Astaire-Rogers movie – opened a nightclub. Clara Bow vacationed right here. She was born in Brooklyn. She was *The It Girl* in 1927. That was the name of the movie she starred in. *It*."

The sun was fast setting behind the city in the west, beyond Brooklyn that bellied out south blocking Byrd's view, but he could see the map and skyline in his mind. The Verrazano Bridge connected Brooklyn to Staten Island, the mainland, and the Mississippi.

Florentine Verrazano had sailed a walnut shell of a French ship *La Dauphine* into the Mahicanituck River in 1524; natives far more robust than the European sailors aboard, watched from the shore as that tide came in.

Mrs. Dalloway Isn't Shallow

"Jane and I thought you were like Mrs. Dalloway."

"That's your Nobel-Prize*itis* flaring up," his younger sister said. "You think you know everything. You misunderstood. Mrs. Dalloway isn't shallow."

"Then life is shallow."

"Don't throw me sops."

"What are sops?" Bruce sneered.

She hadn't attended her sister-in-law's funeral because she and Bruce hadn't spoken for several years. Her move from New York to Vermont hadn't caused their estrangement. It had always been an aspect of their relationship, but she had been able to deny it until their aunt died, the last one of their mother's generation, when Bruce hadn't asked her to stay in one of the two empty bedrooms in his three-bedroom Greenwich Village apartment. When she'd asked, he'd said no.

After the funeral, Jane and Bruce's astronomer daughter had to return to the Keck on Hawaii and their banker son to his young family in London.

Her niece called two weeks later to say that Bruce had not gone back to his lab; according to neighbors and the doormen, he hadn't been out of the apartment. Would retired Aunt please go to NYC and look after him?

So she did.

"Why should I go outside?" Bruce said.

"What good is toothpaste in the tube?"

"As good as shit out of the asshole."

"You think that makes sense?"

That was the battle. When they were children, and Bruce was a young chess master, their father had taken him downtown to Greenwich Village to play the old-timers at the stone tables. Their father would not teach his daughter to play chess because she was a girl, but Bruce allowed her to play with him. When her position bored him, he'd turn the board around and take her side and beat himself.

All these decades later, it wasn't chess. Bruce wasn't turning any boards around on her anymore; he was the one who couldn't make a move.

"What are you doing?"

She was pruning Jane's huge geraniums on the windowsill.

"Don't do that."

"You've got to or they get leggy. You get great sunlight here. They'll bloom all winter. It's only autumn now. Jane kept them beautiful."

The scent of cut geranium hurt. He pressed his chest.

"Is it the Big One? Time to call nine-one-one?"

"Don't do that."

She kept pruning. "Now what?"

"Try to make me feel better."

"With you, it's more like bungee jumping than condolence."

Bruce stood up from the black couch and walked away. That was progress.

A week and a half followed in which she went out every day, down to Battery Park City and up to the Cloisters. She met old friends for lunch behind the Forty-second Street Library in Bryant Park. On the way back to her brother's apartment, she'd pick up groceries at minimarts and feel claustrophobic after decades in suburban supermarkets. She would call her husband in Vermont then cook a light meal for Bruce. She poured him wine. He ate and drank.

"Mommy would have had no patience with this," she said.

"You look like her."

"Mommy weighed one hundred seventy pounds. I weigh one twenty."

She had put on the disk of Beethoven's *Ninth* that she'd brought from home.

"Do you have a Condolence Kit?" he asked.

"You can get them on eBay."

Bruce returned to the black couch facing the window and small terrace. The twenty-story building faced its twin across a wide central garden area. From the twelfth floor, the setting sun was visible. The second movement began *molto vivace*. She sat down on the loveseat facing him.

"Once upon a time a long time ago, when I came home from an exam, there was a candle burning on the kitchen stove, and Mommy told me that Aunt Ruth had died. Daddy had found her in her bath-tub."

"I don't remember."

"Your amnesia about childhood must have freed up all the ROM needed for your scientific triumphs. It explains a lot about you."

"I'm not interested in me."

"What are you interested in?"

"You're right."

"It would be a welcome thing, don't you think, to be able to forget oneself entirely for periods of time? Like taking a vacation from one-self. What a relief that would be. At times, I would so like to drop myself off somewhere."

Bruce laughed. "I'd like to drop you off somewhere, too."

She stifled her joy and went on. "I've thought of that scene a lot, Daddy finding his younger sister's body in the bathtub. Mommy was the one who told the stories, so I don't know if she made it up about Aunt Ruth being engaged to a soldier who died in World War Two or that she had a nervous breakdown in college or that she won writing prizes in high school… that Daddy was valedictorian of his high school class upstate, but it wasn't the same big deal as *you* because there were more than a thousand kids in your class. All those New York City-wide awards."

"So?"

"Any phone calls today?" she tried.

"I don't listen to the machine."

"I wonder if Aunt Ruth just gave up… committed suicide. When Gloria was five and Gilly was just seven months, Jim didn't want a third baby, so I didn't have it. I didn't feel physical pain or the numbness – by definition, I guess – so I was surprised, six months later when I walked and sang with Gloria in her elementary school's Memorial Day Parade. By the time we led the kindergarteners to their checkpoint off Main Street, I felt actually happy. For the first time in six months."

"You never said."

"Most people communicate chiefly by rumor. You and I didn't even do that. You believed the stories Mommy told you about me, and I always knew the stories she told about you: The Hero, The Messiah, The Nobelist… Noble-est."

"I didn't ask you here."

"Times two. But who's counting? I share Mommy's admiration

for you – not the idol worship, but the real deal – for doing the work you do. When I had appendicitis, when I was fourteen, you carried me from the house to the car instead of Daddy. When I was in the hospital for such a long time, you called me from college and sang to me from *The Fantastiks* just like Jerry Orbach."

"Did I?"

"You also phoned me when I told Mommy I was pregnant with Gloria, to say how pleased you and Jane were because you had thought I was too selfish to want to have children. That, after three years of infertility torture."

"I'm sorry."

"So am I."

"Why are you crying?"

She got up and went into the kitchen to busy herself making a pot of tea. There was a pass-through in the wall between the kitchen and living room. She leaned over the sink towards the opening. "I only remember seeing you cry two times, around when you were ten or so, once when you didn't get chosen for a Little League team, the other when you broke your arm playing stick ball. I remember you lying on the couch looking frail, which surprised me, and Mommy calling Daddy at his office, which scared me. Did Daddy set your arm himself?"

"I don't remember."

She passed Bruce a mug of tea. Returning to the living room with her own cup, she took a photo from her pocketbook resting on the piano bench. "I found this before I came down."

In the picture, four grinning teenagers were piled in an uneasy pyramid, two boys as the base, two girls as the second tier, and a third, smallest girl at the apex. They wore bathing suits.

"There we are, the four of us, with Jim's sister on top. Mommy drove us to Jones Beach. Did you even have your driver's license then?"

"I may have, but she liked to drive us."

"Jim's sister, Irene, is a fifty-seven year old divorced mother of a high school freshman."

"Nice picture."

"It's for you. Jane looks so pretty."

"Thanks."

"We were so young. After Gilly was born, breach, the next day, my OB praised me, and I said, 'for what? All I did was survive.' He said, 'for that'."

"Enough!" Bruce protested.

"So we don't get to the *Ode to Joy*. Maybe we'll never hear it again. It's enough that Beethoven could make any music to begin with. Then he went deaf. Now it's enough. *Dayenu*."

"I thought you had given up on religion."

"I'm with Wallace Stevens on the subject of ghosts in the machine."

"Which means?"

"Which means I will stop, but you won't. I'll go back to Vermont tomorrow, but if you don't get moving, I'll be back."

"Is that a threat or a promise?"

"Yes."

Bruce's sweeping gesture took in the room and situation. "This isn't a metaphor."

"How do you know? You're the scientist. You know how hard it is to wheedle any verifiable information out of reality. It's like trying to get you out of this apartment."

He had finished his tea and walked into the kitchen. He spoke through the pass-through. "When the Towers fell, Jane was on Minetta Lane doing a grant evaluation tour. I was in DC doing peer review. Nothing was moving. I couldn't get back to the city. After a few days, I finally got back."

She had called Jane. She knew this story.

"I wish I could go home now." He went into his bedroom.

The next morning, Bruce showered, shaved, and dressed before she awakened. She packed her small bag before venturing into the living room/dining room L. Bruce had brewed a pot of loose tea in a metal ball infuser on a chain hooked to the teapot handle. The mini bran muffins she'd bought were on a plate, and cranberry juice was poured in two small glasses.

"I'll drive you up to Penn Station."

En route to the basement garage, she was relieved to see that everyone they passed in the hallway, elevator, and lobby reacted with familiar NYC behavior: guarded recognition when there was any, self-absorbed indifference the rest of the time. Perhaps the young man in the garage moved more quickly to bring the car around, but it was impossible to know. The uptown drive was silent in the car, city cacophony outside. Bruce pulled up behind the taxi line on the Eighth Avenue side. Instead of a social kiss farewell, she took out the unwrapped gift she'd picked up for him earlier in the week.

"Here, read page sixty-six when you're in the mood."

Bruce looked at the slim paperback. He read the blue cover aloud. "*I Heard God Laughing.* Hafiz?"

She smiled. "You don't know everything, and you're always surprised that I'm not still fifteen, which I can begin to appreciate. I'll email you when I get in."

It was hours later when he looked at page sixty-six of the Ladinsky translation. He'd driven back downtown and parked again in the garage, but then he went for a long walk that took him to his lab where he became absorbed and lost track of time. Refusing to be refused, a colleague took him out for dinner. Back in his apartment alone, Bruce leafed to the page in the book his sister had given him. He heard the medieval Persian poet's words in his sister's voice telling him he was no saint in a chess game with God, whose fabulous move made the saint rejoice and concede. Bruce silently debated and successfully refuted his sister's patronizing conclusion that he believed he still had moves to make. He put the paperback down on a table and walked around the empty apartment to the windowsill, to Jane's freshly pruned geraniums. He rubbed a leaf to release the pungent scent. He felt no saintly laughter rising, but his mouth curved in a smile.

The Man with Ten Hats (June – October, 2004)

On the last day of August, 2004, Marwa al-Hal was one of the two hundred or more protestors arrested during a demonstration outside the GOP Presidential Convention in New York City. In 2012, this mass arrest was ruled illegal. Marwa had been about to begin her junior year as a Presidential Scholar at Fordham, and she was taken into custody with another Presidential Scholar, a senior, her boyfriend James-Beekmans. During the slow interrogation, incarceration, and her sudden, surprise release, Marwa responded to her accuser by politely addressing him as Officer Iblis because Iblis was Satan's Muslim name, and Satan meant 'accuser'. "Officer, I am definitely not an idealist of any kind. I don't have illusions," she said. "I'm one of those people who sees through to nothing."

Marwa's quotation about illusion was from a Flannery O'Connor

about a PhD, whose wooden leg is stolen from her by her Bible salesman lover who leaves her helpless in a barn.

After her 9/11 injury, Marwa's synesthesia hadn't returned with
her eyesight. She saw the world differently and thought, what if her
mother's TV psychic were right, that there was no death; death was
an illusion, a test, but one you were forced to take blindly. That was
how she felt – blind – once her colors were gone. The legless
woman's name had been Joy Hopewell, but she changed her name
to Hulga because it sounded ugly. To Marwa, Hulga sounded like a
character out of *Iceland's Bell* that she'd read over and over three
years before.

Her boyfriend James-Beekmans and most other demonstrators
were not released as quickly as Marwa had been; the Company,
which moved in time as in space, half perceiv'd, half creat'd her future. Everyone called James-Beekmans by both names as if they were
one. He was very tall and very black, and mistaken as a basketball
player for Fordham University, but not for very long after you met
him. James-Beekmans had grown up in a neighborhood near Fordham, Belmont, the Bronx's Little Italy.

"Just west of the Bronx Zoo that I thought belonged to my grandfather because he took me there like daily when I was little."

"You were never little," Marwa replied.

He had grown up fighting and defeating white boys who considered him an alien in their territory, when, as he had explained it to
Marwa, his people had owned and were buried in land in New York

City since the seventeen hundreds.

"You know the South Street Seaport," James-Beekmans asked on their first date back in January. "That Beekman Street? That's us; we're Beekmans. We dropped the master's apostrophe three hundred years ago. We moved north into Manhattan woods and swamp before Olmsted started terraforming Central Park, and we were run out of there when that real estate became worth something, but once we were in the Bronx, we stood our ground. My mom's grandfather took photos of the Italians when they first arrived, and he delivered mail to the ones who could read."

James-Beekmans and Marcus got along fine when Marwa introduced her Stuyvesant High classmate to her boyfriend on a hot Sunday at the beginning of August when Marcus was in the city for the weekend, down from Cambridge.

"Why don't you just say Harvard?" Marwa said.

Marcus had the September *Scientific American* in his hand. James-Beekmans said, "You ever wonder why the September issue comes out at the beginning of August?"

Marcus looked at the cover. "All the time."

Marwa took the magazine out of Marcus' hand and riffled through it to a dog-eared page and paraphrased, "According to Einstein, gravity arises from the geometry of spacetime. Any huge weight leaves an imprint he described in a 1915 equation. The weight of the earth causes time to move more rapidly for a fruit near the top of a tree than for a scientist in its shade."

Marwa paused, her eyes having cast ahead, and she scanned the next words more slowly, murmuring aloud. "When the apple falls, that's because time is warping."

The three undergraduates were standing on the esplanade at Battery Park City looking west over the Hudson. Marwa turned her head briefly towards the great absence of the Towers. Both young men translated her glance. Marcus quickly drew Marwa's attention back to the article's authors and said he was hoping to do grad work with the one at Berkeley, "on the holographic principle, relating space-time geometry to information content."

Later, Marwa mistakenly thought that James-Beekmans had liked Marcus for always answering a question with another question, but it was because Marcus had in that moment distracted her from falling bodies, her memory of escaping with her younger brother Joey from his elementary school near Stuyvesant High.

Marwa handed him the magazine back. "I'm not into science so much anymore since my colors are gone."

Marcus laughed. "Yeah, you're into James-Beekmans."

"This one's going to the real Cambridge." She patted his dark forearm. "All expenses paid on a Gates magic carpet."

Marcus looked impressed at the mention of the new scholarship, Bill Gates' American answer to the primo British Rhodes.

"I'm applying for one," James-Beekmans corrected.

"When's the deadline for that?" Marcus asked.

"You've got to be a senior," Marwa explained.

"Duh," Marcus said.

"November first," James-Beekmans answered, "for a Master's."

"In…?" Marcus said.

"Anthro."

"Biological Anthropology. James-Beekmans is going to be an anthropological geneticist after medical school."

"Are you sure you aren't Jewish?" Marcus teased. "You sound just like my mother."

The threesome had walked in the direction of the ongoing building of a new 'Teardrop Park' on the esplanade, and looked down through the fencing at the hardhat workers pouring concrete, at the arranged boulders and another crew of workers planting trees and small shrubs. Leaning against the protective fence for a better look was Joey's friend Ositadimma Bem. The boy recognized Marwa and grinned upward at the height of James-Beekmans. The child gestured basketball dribbling and shooting.

"Hey, Marwa, this park is gonna be so great!"

"Watch out you don't fall in before it even opens," Marwa scolded.

Marcus picked up several loose stones near Ositadimma's feet. He juggled them to distract the boy, moving him away from the fence altogether.

"Can you do more?" Ositadimma asked.

"Try me." Marcus angled one palm to receive one, two, three more stones. He was juggling six when one dropped, and he hissed a curse, surprising James-Beekmans. Ositadimma quickly picked up the stone and tossed it back to Marcus, who was keeping the other five in the air. This time, Marcus kept all six up, down and sideways for several minutes. Ositadimma whistled admiration.

"How d'you do that?"

Marcus caught the stones and tossed one to the boy. "You can do that, right?"

Ositadimma tossed it hand to hand easily, impatiently. Marcus put three stones in his shorts pocket and tossed two back and forth, hand to hand, keeping their height level. He threw one to Ositadimma, and the boy imitated.

Marcus called for the two back and juggled three. "You watching?"

"Gimme."

Ositadimma again imitated the pace and arc.

"You want four?" Marcus asked.

"For later." The boy concentrated. He stopped juggling and held the stones in one hand, reaching out for the remaining three which Marcus gave him.

"Try using balls of the same size and weight instead of stones," Marcus suggested.

Ositadimma nodded. "There's a lot more to this."

"Just stay clear of the fence," Marcus said. "Don't lean on it."

Ositadimma ignored the warning. Marcus, Marwa, and James-Beekmans watched the neophyte walking away, trying to juggle at the same time.

"He'll have Joey doing that now, thank you very much," Marwa sighed. "Something you picked up at Harvard?"

"The masters are at Caltech. It's not really the number you keep in the air, it's the throwing sequences that are interesting. There's only one law, no matter what the tempo, one hand can make only one throw at a time. You can increase the height of one throw in a sequence so long as you equally decrease the height of another throw that lands later, but you have to know how much later, or—"

"Or else."

"Well, you asked."

Walking back to the reopened Chambers Street subway to return to their various locations uptown and in the Bronx, Marwa talked about Joey and Ositadimma Bem, how his Nigerian name meant 'May things change for the better or be better from today and forever'. "Bem means peace."

"Sounds like that song from *Norma Rae*," Marcus said.

"Would that you had your ukulele with you," Marwa teased.

In response, Marcus started singing the movie's hopeful lyric.

"Good thing you're a mathematician," James-Beekmans said.

"Oh, Marcus knows all the Academy Award-winning songs," Marwa said. "What year was that?"

"1979."

"*To Kill A Mockingbird* was 1962," James-Beekmans offered. "That's the only one I know the year of."

"*Days of Wine and Roses* was '62. I only know the songs."

"He knows them in order from 1934," Marwa said. "Please don't get him started."

That night back at the beginning of August, when Marwa and James-Beekmans had returned from meeting Marcus, they went to dinner at his parents' home in the Bronx. Inside the row house it was air-conditioned against the humid heat, but the two were sitting outside on back steps that overlooked a small, neatly planted garden and driveway, part of a common space of garages and gardens behind the attached homes. Marwa's wavy hair was twisted and barretted up on her head. James-Beekmans stroked away some shine of sweat from her long, lovely neck and played with the wetness between his thumb and first finger. His touch evoked an involuntary purring sound from Marwa's larynx. Shocked, she dropped the draft of his Gates personal statement essay she had been reading. Picking it up, she cleared her throat.

"What's wrong?" James-Beekmans said.

"Nothing. 'The Hobbit and Goliath' is a great title. It's great the way you put them together and then together with blond mummies in China with tattoos. I didn't know about these early hominid migrations to Indonesia, South Africa, China. I love the Cherchen Man." She searched a page. "A tattooed woman with red yarn pierced earrings who was over six feet tall, and he was 6'6" with ten hats. Ten Hats!" Marwa stopped. "Do you have to go to med school to be a geneticist, anthropological or otherwise?"

"You ask my mother that question, but wait till I'm out of earshot." He imitated his mother's voice, "'Your father and I haven't commuted our asses to Twenty-third Street to a VA Hospital for three decades for you to—"

"Spare me her colorful language."

"What did Marcus swear when he was juggling?" James-Beekmans asked.

"Heat-waste!"

"Do any of you Stuy kids ever say anything that's not an allusion?"

"Probably not. It's from a sci fi story, *Spell My Name With An S* by Asimov. These energy beings without bodies change a nuclear physicist's career, his whole life, just by changing the first letter of his name from Z to S."

"Heat-waste?"

"I guess to pure energy beings, heat-waste is obscene."

"Spelling our last name without that slave apostrophe was a big deal."

"My last name is my father's. I like the way they do it in Norway, I think. A girl gets her mother's name with *dottir* as a suffix, and a boy gets his father's with son…Oh, it's so hot!"

Marwa pulled her damp skirt free from where it was sticking to her behind and the backs of her legs.

"Heat outdoors, parents indoors. Candide's choice?"

"Do you ever say anything that's not an allusion?"

"The past dies last in language."

"Who said that?" Marwa brightened.

"I just did. So what should I call you? A nickname? *Ekename* in Old English just means 'another name.' Crossword puzzle; I had to look it up."

"So what d'you want to call me?"

"What d'you want to call me?"

Marwa blushed. Then James-Beekmans stood up, took her in his arms, and kissed her.

Manufactured Goods

The ancient Greeks had two words for time, chronos and kairos. Chronos refers to sequential, measurable time, and kairos to moments of hope and possibility. Kairos also means weather in both ancient and modern Greek, and the plural, καιροι, kairoi or keri, means the times.

On Sputnik's launch date, October 4, 1957, Uncle Theo's body was found in the East River off the Greenpoint Piers. Had he jumped or been dumped off one of them? He was notable even among Hayleys for his movie star looks and his Thanksgiving grace: "Let us give thanks for Aristotle's School at Mieza, where he educated Alexander, the ingrate who later berated his teacher for making public knowledge that The Great thought best kept exclusive to the elite. Now dig in!"

Uncle Theo, a naval lieutenant in WWII, eschewed the military. He was called to sea via personal history, not Pearl Harbor. "Hayleys always sail." Surviving the war, he became a copywriter for a major NYC radio station where he met his first wife and thereafter was an early TV producer, creating *The Howdy Doody Show.* He often packed its Peanut Gallery with nephews, nieces, and his two daughters Thalia and Thorne. Principals of the *Howdy* show included Princess Summerfallwinterspring, who did nothing for him; he thought Claribel the clown was a sadist. Uncle Theo also became an alcoholic, which for some time enhanced his irresistible charm. That was a common delusion until Dudley Moore's *Arthur* movies collided with an increasing prohibition-health consciousness decades later.

In 1937, when Theo was fifteen, his father had him called out of prep school class in Connecticut where they were at the climax of *Huck Finn* – "All right then, I'll go to hell!" – with the news of his maternal grandfather's sudden death on the golf course.

"Take the train down to the city and out to Brooklyn, and I'll drive us back up to Mystic. I have something to tell you." This circular route made no sense to Theo, but life was increasingly appearing to him as Ezekiel's wheels within wheels.

On the last leg of the trip, as they passed Rye Playland, his father suddenly pulled off the road at an exit. A police car followed them.

"You can't stop here," the cop began writing a ticket.

"Please, Officer, I'm telling my son that his mother has left us for another man." Theo's father named the man.

Inured to scenes of greater catastrophe, the policeman nevertheless relented and left them with a warning.

After the funeral, Theo's mother was inconsolable. When Theo went to her bedroom to try, she spoke wildly. "My father was a giant! Hit by lightning, a thunderbolt! Struck down by jealous gods! A creator! A Hayley! He inherited forests, the lumber business, industrialized silk – invented the machines, built the factories – the Japanese Emperor gave my father a medal! One of the trinity creating Mystic Seaport! He employed the family's men and men in two states – Theo, you must always be a gentleman," she choked. "You are not your father's son. I was raped, and you are a rapist's son, but you are a Hayley!"

Theo recoiled. He listened to his mother's ragged breathing. Then he heard himself exhale, icing his respiration into the words: "Never need worry, Mother. I'm also a queer."

She shut her Gorgon eyes, but Theo had not been turned to stone. Leaving that room, he felt surprise and relief. He'd spoken a truth he'd only known as nameless fear, and now seeing it, it was so much smaller than its nightmare form that he felt like laughing. He also felt nauseated and his stomach ached, as if he'd vomited, but of all the things he'd just learned – about his grandfather's ludicrous death by golf, his mother's victimized life, his alleged paternity, the divorce – the thing that mattered most was what he now knew about himself. "All right then, I'll go to hell!" Theo felt better.

Why, wondered his nephew Rob in 2011, had Uncle Theo's last

sea journey been in the East River as a corpse? In the midst of the patriarch's death and his daughter's hysterical first divorce consistent with the Hayley tradition of serial marriages rather than murders, when the NYPD labeled Uncle Theo a suicide, no one had cared to investigate. Rob's two cousins, Thalia and Thorne, Uncle Theo's only children, had been scattered to backwaters in Bermuda and the Isle of Wight by their own marital escapades and didn't share Rob's curiosity, piqued when Thalia self-published a Hayley family history that hardly included her father as a footnote.

"There's a reason dogs don't chase parked cars," she emailed Rob, recently retired from four decades as a Connecticut College English professor: 'How sharper than a serpent's tooth,' came instantly to Rob's mind, along with revived memories of Uncle Theo – in Manhattan, at *The Howdy Doody Show*; in Uncle Theo's Bartleby-like room in the family lumber business building in Brooklyn; sailing on the thirty-four foot *Kairos* in the sound off the Connecticut coast in the summers; how handsome Uncle Theo was, how heliotropic.

Rob had only seen Uncle Theo drunk once, one Thanksgiving before he married second wife Laura, the black woman he brought to his mother's house for dinner. Grandmother Hayley and Rob's mother had each taken an elbow of Laura's and led her away from Uncle Theo who was left to the men – to do what? Rob remembered only the image of the two white women at the beautiful black woman's elbows, but he knew that after alcoholism ended his TV career and second marriage, Uncle Theo had gone on the wagon.

There had been at least two holiday seasons when Uncle Theo had been the life of the parties solo and sober, sipping limed soda or ginger ale in a champagne flute. Uncle Theo had gone to work for Rob's father in the Brooklyn lumber business. "Your Uncle Theo could sell a pile of twisted lumber to a seasoned salesman – snow to the Eskimos!" The two city blocks on the waterfront in Greenpoint were the last remnant of the Hayley empire begun three centuries before that had consumed Adirondack forests stolen from Mohawks who had ironically named the area *Ratirontaks*, insulting the also indigenous Algonquins for 'eating trees' when food was scarce. The Dutch had transliterated the word *Aderondackx*. This information was included in Thalia's history: "The Hayleys developed, defended, and defined eighteenth and nineteenth century America and are dedicated to remember it in the twentieth and twenty-first. Northeastern forests cut down in the eighteenth and nineteenth centuries regrew when farm fields were abandoned. The region is now one of the most important for carbon storage on the planet."

Another 1957 memory: Thorne had run away from home in Stonington to Rob's parents' house in Mystic. Rob's mother called him at prep school in Virginia as he packed for Thanksgiving.

"Maybe you can calm her down," Rob's mother said. "She listens to you."

She put Thorne on the phone. Rob could hardly make out what she was running on about – what? Sputnik?

"'Where does God live now?' my mother asked! She is an idiot!

Now how can I live there?"

Rob didn't remember what he'd told his cousin, but it must've been some Southern prep school paternoster about the necessity of forgiving the older generation for the sins they'd inherited and passed down. 'Forgive us our trespasses, as we forgive them that trespass against us.' Rob knew that's what he was telling himself at that pivotal time in his adolescence when Uncle Theo had just died.

This October day in 2011, Rob was sailing the inherited *Kairos* out of New London where he had lived for a quarter century with Isaac, who like Uncle Theo's Laura, was black. Isaac, ten years Rob's junior, was a professor in the Art Department at Connecticut College where Rob was *emeritus* in English. Isaac was leaning back, warm in the sun, as memories of Uncle Theo prompted Rob. "He built a model plane with a real engine mounted behind a real propeller and promised, 'We're going to take this baby out and make her soar!' And we did..."

Rob squinted at the autumn sun. "Ask Ptolemy and Copernicus what the Sun's relationship is to Earth, you get two different answers. One's a false, failed assumption about reality. Henry Adams' essay on energy and economy: *The Virgin and the Dynamo...* was Great Grandfather Hayley a dynamo and we're... what are we now? Batteries?"

Isaac, familiar with Rob's rhetorical wanderlust, kept his eyes closed and enjoyed the swell from the wake of the Cross Sound ferry lift and lower the *Kairos*. Now he opened them and followed Rob's celestial squint.

"Never bad weather out of a Watteau sky," Isaac admired.

"My father was married seven times. And us – not even once."

As the sailboat heeled over, Isaac fingers glossed through small white-cresting swells.

Rob saw Isaac's gesture. "Foam's an accidental excrescence of the sea, probably another one of those fractal iterations of the minute three to five percentage of the Universe that we're supposed to be."

Isaac raised his hand and flicked water at Rob. "Ashes to ashes, foam to foam."

Rob brought the boat about; Isaac assisted. Heading home, they were quiet, listening to the sails, water, and seabirds. Close to the marina, tightening his grip on the tiller, Rob continued his interior monologue out loud.

"The summer I was fifteen, I was on the *Kairos*, right at that cove." Rob pointed, "…with Uncle Theo. He told me about Lord Byron and Lukas. He quoted, 'Love dwells not in our will. Nor can I blame thee, though it be my lot, to strongly, wrongly, vainly love thee still.' Byron let meter force a lie,' Uncle Theo said, 'Nothing wrongly there, kid. It's just the times.'"

"Was that a proposal before?"

"It's about time."

It was a hot night in October, not Indian summer because though there had been chilly days, there had been no frost so far. Still, it was a night that belonged to summer, not autumn, and the inconsistent weather was to blame for the awful cold Theo had. Shocked out of a nightmare of choking, he had awakened in his small room in the lumberyard. He couldn't breathe. Groggy with sleep and panic, he groped around in the bathroom for Miltown and Dristan. He stripped off sweat-soaked pajamas and dressed; he had to get some air.

He walked two blocks to the nearest pier, shaking his head to clear it of the thick humid clouds that also blackened the sky. How could it be so hot in October? Had that Russian satellite affected the weather? He could feel the pill start to work. Pills? The Dristan made his heart race, but the Miltown dulled fear into the placid observation that he might have taken too many of either – or both.

Then he fell, suddenly and wholly underwater into high tide. For a moment, the shock was joy, and he was a boy back in Mystic, leaping off the dock to cool off on summer nights. The cold October current numbed him now. 'E'en in the gasp of death, love dwells not in our will…' It was so dark that he didn't know if his eyes were open or closed… he didn't care. It didn't matter. 'O dear, what can the matter be, dear, dear, what can the matter be, O dear, what can the matter be, Theo's so long at the fair.' He was falling back to sleep, and in the distance he could see his sister's lovely boy sailing on open seas…

On Christmas Eve, Rob and Isaac were married in an evening

ceremony in Rob's lifelong trust fund friend's glass-walled condo on an upper floor in a high-rise in Williamsburgh just south of the Greenpoint Piers.

Looking out at the East River and lower Manhattan skyline, their hostess apologized, "It's a shame it's not summertime. We could've used the roof terrace."

She was dressed in white mink-collared and cuffed red velvet like Rosemary Clooney in *White Christmas*, and some of the guests were similarly camped up in seasonal costumes, as gifts or sugar plums, candy canes, or elves.

"You couldn't have hired two Rockettes and four wooden soldiers in June," Rob thanked, hugging her. "Here is the perfect space and time."

Although wintry months lay ahead, the wedding ceremony was an expression of the hopeful solstice as in the northern hemisphere its holidays are. The couple's vows, an amalgam of tradition and novelty, were applauded heartily by everyone there and by an avuncular one wherever.

The Reckoning Ball

Mr. Bitelli...is a sixty year old Brooklynite, born in Italy in 1900, the owner of the candy store/luncheonette.

Charlayne...is a fourteen year old African-American, daily customer at Bitelli's on her way home from school.

Doctor Stern...is Mr. Bitelli's age, a Jewish refugee of a dozen years, a physician at a local hospital. She walks to Bitelli's every Tuesday for eggs.

At rise, it is a wintry Tuesday late afternoon, February 23, 1960, near Ebbets Field, Brooklyn, N.Y. In Bitelli's Luncheonette, MR. BITELLI unnecessarily wipes off some of the framed photos of Dodgers greats like Zach Wheat and Pee Wee Reese. Then he turns, takes a clean cloth, gives the immaculate counter a once over, and serves CHARLAYNE a donut. Behind the counter is a mirrored wall of glass shelves appointed with other framed photos, dessert glasses, soda ads, a few Valentine's hearts left over from the recent holiday, etc., and a radio playing a medley of Sinatra hits. The counter runs along SR wall, catty-cornered so that the upstage glass wall looks onto the street, and the luncheonette's name is arched over the glass. Small tables and chairs are centered; the store entrance is USL. DSL is a public telephone booth, the immediate and constant object of CHARAYNE'S attention. She is a pretty fourteen year old, mature for her age. She wears a skirt, sweater, socks and saddle shoes. Her school books are on the counter stool beside her. MR. BITELLI is dressed in a clean white tee shirt and wrap-around white apron. He is agitated, glad of CHARLAYNE'S presence as a distraction. He has a thick Italian accent; DOCTOR STERN is Viennese. The dialogue is periodically punctuated by the sound of a one-ton iron ball hitting long-standing cement, a block away. All action must stop momentarily at each thud.

(THUD)

MR. BITELLI: *(turns down the radio)* You got much homework?

CHARLAYNE: What? Oh, yeah. Bio and math.

(MR. BITELLI serves her cocoa.)

(THUD)

(MR. BITELLI spills some of the cocoa)

CHARLAYNE: What's the matter?

MR. BITELLI: Didn't you hear that?

CHARLAYNE: What? *(turning)* Not the phone—

MR. BITELLI: No. *(touches his head)* All day now, me and

Brooklyn, we got a pounding headache.

CHARLAYNE: Yeah, I know.

MR. BITELLI: You're so smart, Charlayne. You know what the President says when they bombed Pearl Harbor?

CHARLAYNE: 'Today is a day that will live in infamy—'

MR. BITELLI: Okay, you learn somethin' in that school. 'Live in infamy.' Again, today.

CHARLAYNE: When did Japan build a new military? They're not allowed.

MR. BITELLI: (*Pointing out the window*) They're tearin' it down, they're tearin' the heart outta my chest, the heart outta Brooklyn.

(*THUD*)

CHARLAYNE: (*Kind*) Oh, Ebbets Field; they have a brass band in there. A lot of us went in on the way out of school. They're letting anyone in today who wants to because it's the last day. A couple a'hundred people; it looked empty.

(*DOCTOR STERN enters; the glass door jingles. CHARLAYNE rushes to the phone, realizes it was the door, turns.*)

Some of the old players were there, and you know what? The flag's flying upside down in center field.

MR. BITELLI: What you waitin' for so hard, Charlayne? Let me get you another cocoa. You're like a— (*singing the melody and gesturing as CHARLAYNE returns to her stool*)

CHARLAYNE: —Jack in the box?

MR. BITELLI: Pop goes the weasel. (*To DOCTOR STERN*) Doctor Stern, your Tuesday sabbatical from the hospital?

DOCTOR STERN: (*taking off her coat, a doc-tor's white jacket beneath, sitting at the counter*) Constitutional? Yes, Mr. Bitelli. What flag is flying upside down? That's the international signal for distress.

CHARLAYNE: In Ebbets Field, Doctor Stern. The flag's flying upside down. They said it was by accident.

(THUD)

MR. BITELLI: What's that, distress?

CHARLAYNE: Like an S.O.S.

(*The following dialogue is a pattern that BITELLI and STERN repeat weekly:*)

DOCTOR STERN: Do you have fresh eggs today, Mr. Bitelli?

MR. BITELLI: How you like 'em? You want 'em fried, scrambled, poached, hard-boiled, soft-boiled, over easy, or maybe an omelet?

DOCTOR STERN: Surprise me.

MR. BITELLI: I'll surprise you. Tea in a glass or maybe coffee?

DOCTOR STERN: Thank you, coffee.

(THUD)

MR. BITELLI: (*He gets cup, pours coffee, makes eggs/toast.*) You know who's over there right now? (*He touches the radio behind him, the source of this information.*) Roy Campanella, they said. He caught the last ball thrown at Ebbets Field, and now he's in a wheel-chair.

CHARLAYNE: The crane is bigger than the tyrannosaurus rex in the Museum of Natural History.

MR. BITELLI: Big head on that rex, like my Uncle Carmine. (*gestures*) I bet the ground shook when that dinosaur put its foot down, (*reminiscent*) like my Uncle Carmine.

(THUD)

CHARLAYNE: The iron ball, they got it painted like a big baseball.

MR. BITELLI: Don't tell me about it! I was 14 years old when I come to this country, and the first thing I remember I see after the Statue of Liberty (*he crosses himself reverently*), my Uncle Carmine took me to this, this – castle – with a lobby like a grand opera house, with the floor marble from Italy, the chandelier musta been diamonds – (*pause*) Ebbets Field! And the green grass field, for an Emperor! When that iron ball painted like a big baseball hit the Visitors' Dugout – (*touches radio again*) that's what they said got it first – it hits me right here. (*he strikes his chest*) I look like I'm still standing, but I'm dead. It's too late for me. 1960. I'm sixty years old. I'm born—

CHARLAYNE: (*This record's also been played many times before*) January 1st, 1900, I know, we all know, all Brooklyn knows. You saw it all.

(THUD)

MR. BITELLI: I seen Zach Wheat in Ebbets Field. .317 lifetime, over .300 in fourteen of nineteen major league seasons. Double figures in triples in the dead-ball era, seven times before 1920! He was .461 in 1916. I wish I never live long enough to see today.

CHARLAYNE: The dead-ball era?

MR. BITELLI: (*to DOCTOR STERN*) Youth. (*to CHARLAYNE*) Before they put cork in the ball, you hit it – (*with vocal raspberry, gestures straight, then abrupt drop*).

DOCTORSTERN: I will be sixty also, in July.

MR. BITELLI: We seen a lot. Zach Wheat. In '31, they added the double-decker stands to left field and center field and the scoreboard moved from behind the left field fence to right field. I was thirty-one years old.

DOCTOR STERN: I started practicing medicine in Vienna. This wasn't so easy for a woman.

MR. BITELLI: They tear down Ebbets Field, they might as well tear this place down. (*about CHARLAYNE*) She's gonna be a doctor one day. Some head on her. (*to CHARLAYNE*) So, what's on the telephone you waitin' so hard to hear? Harvard calling you already?

CHARLAYNE: I'm only a freshman. A boy said he would call me after practice. He said he would.

(THUD)

They said it's going to take ten weeks to tear it all down.

MR. BITELLI: Ten weeks? What boy?

CHARLAYNE: He's six foot seven.

MR. BITELLI: He tell you that? I don't care how many feet he's got so long he keeps his two hands to himself. (*Placing platter in front of DOCTOR STERN*) You gotta break the eggs to make the omelet. How's the hospital?

DOCTOR STERN: I delivered twins this morning – a girl and a boy. They named them Esau and Rachel.

MR. BITELLI: Good for you!

(THUD)

My business – it goes with that reckoning ball.

CHARLAYNE: Wrecking ball.

MR. BITELLI: That's what I said.

CHARLAYNE: They're scouting him, and he's only a sophomore.

MR. BITELLI: Scouting him for what?

CHARLAYNE: *(Exasperated)* For basketball. Basketball. That's the game of the future. He wants to play with Bill Russell and the Celtics, in Boston.

DOCTOR STERN: *(Eating)* Mmm… delicious.

CHARLAYNE: I like hamburgers betters.

MR. BITELLI: All your taste is in your mouth. In Boston. Basketball. Hmph.

(THUD)

(He puts a hamburger patty on the griddle.)

CHARLAYNE: No, hamburger.

MR.BITELLI: You hear the sizzle?

DOCTOR STERN: She's listening for the phone, not sizzles. (*To CHARLAYNE*) How old are you?

CHARLAYNE: Fourteen and a half.

DOCTOR STERN: And a half. Yes, at fourteen, we go by halves, waiting for the telephone to ring, for a boy to call. It's a good idea, to live life by halves.

(THUD)

CHARLAYNE: You certainly like eggs.

DOCTOR STERN: There was a time I dreamed about them for a long time.

MR. BITELLI: All my dreams are in Ebbets Field.

CHARLAYNE: Oh, Mr. Bitelli, it's just a building! They tear them down, they build a new one. The Dodgers are in Los Angeles now. That's American. You've got to go with the flow. Change that radio dial from Sinatra to Fats Domino.

MR. BITELLI: Frank Sinatra is a saint.

CHARLAYNE: (*sad*) I guess he's not going to call after all.

(THUD)

MR. BITELLI: Don't go lighting a candle for Mr. Basketball yet. (*Remembering*) In 1955, they turned off the lights in Ebbets Field… Thirty-three thousand of us held up lighted matches, all of us standing in the dark with, like, candles – for Pee Wee Reese's thirty-sixth birthday. 'The Little Colonel!' He was shortstop since 1940, fifteen years except for the war years. I burned my fingers holding that match. It was an honor. Pee Wee Reese.

DOCTOR STERN: (*avoiding the war years*, to *CHARLAYNE*) How is your father doing?

CHARLAYNE: (*receiving hamburger, putting on ketchup*) Thank you. They moved him to the IRT up in Queens. The last station stop is called Flushing. Doesn't that sound disgusting? Flushing? But he says it's nice up there.

DOCTOR STERN: You make it sound as if it is a foreign country.

CHARLAYNE: It is. It's Queens. I just hope he doesn't expect us to move. (*She eyes the telephone booth longingly, then eats as a distraction.*)

DOCTOR STERN: (*laughs*) Moving isn't such a bad thing, except maybe to Los Angeles.

MR. BITELLI: You don't understand. I saw Jackie Robinson steal third base off the Cardinals, July 26, 1950, ten years ago.

CHARLAYNE: (*gestures a time-out*) Mr. Bitelli, enough! You and that iron ball pounding, if I hear any more of your stories—

DOCTOR STERN: Today is the story you'll tell a teenager waiting for the phone to ring one day. (*It is getting dark outside*)

(*THUD*)

MR. BITELLI: (*Grateful to DOCTOR STERN*) Tommy Glaviano is at third, and Dusty Boggess is the umpire at second where (*for CHARLAYNE, who groans, then laughs*) Carl Furillo slid in on the back end of a double steal! No, no, you laugh, but listen, in 1947, yes, the Dodgers lost the World Series to the Yankees (*he pretends to spit*), but the point is, in game four, when the Dodgers are down two games to one and desperately need a win, Carl Furillo draws a one-out walk. Pinch runner Al Gionfriddo steals second and pinch hitter Pete Reiser is walked on purpose, despite he's the winning run. Cookie Lavagetto pinch hits for Eddie Stanky, and the second pitch, Lavagetto belts it off the right field wall, driving in the tying and winning runs. (*Breathes out, post-coital. Then, remembering CHAR-LAYNE'S boyfriend, an expression of disgust*) Basketball! The game of the future! (*DOCTOR STERN lifts up her coffee cup for a refill; her coat sleeve falls slightly, revealing the blue tattooed number on her wrist. CHARAYNE has seen it before but never asked...*)

CHARLAYNE: Did it hurt?

(THUD)

DOCTOR STERN: (*as MR. BITELLI pours coffee*) Yes. (*She reaches out her arm*) Don't be afraid. It won't hurt you. (*CHARLAYNE touches the tattoo.*)

CHARLAYNE: They cut off the right foot of slaves who ran away. (*The phone rings. She runs to the phone.*) Hello? (*Listens, ecstatic reaction*) Yeah, I was waiting. No, I really was. (*Turns back and continues muffled, happy conversation.*)

(The last THUD, this time with the sound of much glass and metal breaking)

MR. BITELLI: There she goes. (*hand on his chest. DOCTOR STERN ignores this and looks distracted, shaking her head. MR. BITELLI comes out from around the counter and stands beside her, facing out at Ebbets Field, and pats her shoulder.*) Doctor Stern? You okay?

DOCTOR STERN: One of the twins died. Esau – the one born first. (*leaves money on the counter, stands. Before MR. BITELLI can say anything, CHARLAYNE emerges from the phone booth, exultant.*) Good news?

CHARLAYNE: (*Fairly dancing to her books on the stool, putting on her coat, picking up her books, exiting out the door that rings*) The best! He's meeting me at home! We're doing homework together! See you tomorrow, Mr. Bitelli! (*Exits, waves from outside through the glass storefront.*)

MR. BITELLI: (*Thoughtful*) Tomorrow. It's dark. (*About the demolition*) They have to stop now.

DOCTOR STERN: (*Also exiting*) Tomorrow it will be light. They'll start again. So, next Tuesday – surprise me.

MR. BITELLI: I'll surprise you.

(*She nods, exits, the door jingling. DOCTOR STERN waves from outside the window as CHARLAYNE did. MR. BITELLI goes behind the counter, picks up the money left there, and turns up Sinatra who is singing* I'll See You Again. *Listening to the lyrics, fade to black.*)

Gottesman's Constant

Nature is a con artist that uses misdirection as deftly as sleight-of-hand to keep the thing moving and hidden, but at some cost, genius can beat the shell game. Michael Gottesman of Isle End, six foot three, light-haired and blue-eyed, feels covert glances reach like antennae to touch him. The New York airport is so crowded it resembles an anthill.

He walks, aware of moving within a moving pattern. It is altogether too much to bear, yet he is bearing it. The weight of the thing crushes where it is minutely held. It would not have been wrong, merely inadequate, to say he was maddened by it, which includes: Wecj, Peggy, Tyler. He balks at her entirely, yearns to flee east to the tip of the Island to Isle End, the porous land in the water where the earth gives way to sea: Home.

Michael is walking across an airport lobby. A voice announces departures. He walks in his mind back into the spaces of early ado-lescence. On a dark blue night on Isle End, the sky was neatly printed with constellations. Orion was above him and a girl's body beneath him. He liked the smallness of females and his own increasing size in an expanding universe. His neck aches as he walks across the air-port lobby. His throat burns, his mouth is suddenly dry. There are tears in his eyes and he wants his mother.

The sun is setting. A rim of orange light lines the horizon. Fluid layers of sky darken into a spectrum blue to black. Michael stands outside the airport lobby on a taxi line. He ignores people in line in front and behind him, jostling and dropping parts of themselves. He fixes his sight on the bright horizon line and senses the lowering tem-perature and the low tide taste of the air. It is La Guardia Airport, October, 1987. A summer day changes into a winter night with the descent of the sun. The wind blows through his thin jacket, cold against his face. He opens the taxi door and settles inside. He has no destination, but he knows an address in Greenwich Village. Tyler's family had one of their houses there.

Michael looks out the taxi window at the city lights reflecting in the water. The river is Nature, an arm slipping out of a dark cloak of earth – woman. Peggy tightened her lips, and something changed in her eyes. The bridge dips down and attaches itself to land. The taxi stops at a light. The driver leans toward the meter to check his fare. He lights a cigarette. The sulfurous flash, the sharp scent, startles Michael. He is scared. He wants his mother, but he leans back into the car seat. He is hungry. It is a problem to solve, which is all right; Michael solves problems.

The taxi stops because Michael has directed it past Tyler's townhouse south to where the river meets the ocean in an open bay. Money is exchanged. Michael breathes the driver's cigarette smoke into his lungs. It tastes like autumn bonfires.

It's dark below Wall Street late at night, but Michael is unaware of his danger and finds a diner, a crevice to crawl into for food. He eats. It makes him feel better than he has for hours since he confronted Wecj then boarded the shuttle from Boston. The beat of rock music is coming out of a small speaker hooked up in a corner. Beer turns to heat in Michael's blood – he unzips the wind-breaker. They don't know who they have right here in their midst – the old cosmological key. No, the young one. Michael buys a pack of gum, leaves the diner, and walks down dark streets toward the smell of the river.

She had left soon after his birth. He got an awful lot of mothering mileage out of that one from other women and their daughters.

Michael stands at the water's edge and looks into the darkness. The only light reflected in the many-faceted water comes from weak blue streetlamps and distant stars on a moonless night. You are supposed to be modern, proud the old lady had so much blood in her, but those are just words when it's your mother and she left you in diapers.

Michael wishes he had some grass to smoke at the water's edge. He doesn't mind the cold wind blowing his hair into his eyes. It is too long because Peggy wouldn't cut it. Who is finished with him? His mother, Wecj, Peggy, Tyler. Grass makes him think of Tyler. Michael hears footsteps behind him. He turns his head and sees an old bum approach him unsteadily, palm up. Michael takes out what loose change he can finger in his pocket and gives it to the man.

Tyler and he were friends based on topics in astrophysics/meta-mathematics. They loved the same things, QED, each other. Tyler had survived the VN War, was years older than Michael. He wore a sailor's cap folded down and came from Newport, his home more a museum than a place to live. Michael was disoriented the entire weekend in Rhode Island except when they talked physics. Who mentioned homosexuality?

"I'm not like that." Who said that?

So much grass – lost in the smoke… and found. Wecj and Peggy were both jealous and wrong about Tyler.

Michael turns abruptly – something is falling.

Tyler jumped off a bridge. He walked off it as if he were walking from one room to another. Paste that in the scrapbook. Michael nods to himself. The boy's off his rocker, right off the front porch at twenty years old.

Michael turns. In the edge of a shadow outside the streetlight circumference, two drunks fight. They lift their arms heavily and land punches by chance. They grunt, wheeze, and spit. They fall to the ground and quiver on their backs like beetles. They rise again, and bone thuds onto bone, a sound like a lead ball hitting sacks of flour.

Michael goes toward them, yells – a hollow bellow rises from their throats. He slips between them, grabs each one with a fist, then strains to separate them like two halves of a wishbone. It is harder than he thought. They both swing at him. One connects, and Michael falls. Then one of them falls beside him, stinking, and the victor lopes, cursing. Michael raises himself to his knees. He looks at the bum beside him. The man is wrinkled, yellow, and splotched, and has blood on his face, hands, clothes. Michael's eyes are wet. He looks up from the river to the sky. The bum sucks in his snot as he comes to. Michael offers him a stick of gum.

He starts to explain the thing he has discovered or created – they are the same thing: a symmetry of efforts.

"In the beginning was vacuum, but not as we commonly define the word. This is a vacuum we are speaking of which is a symmetry of forces, as for example, when you're underwater whichever direction you look in the water appears the same. In other words, the evolution of the universe as we know it begins, before the beginning or big bang, in this vacuum which experienced a kind of asymmetrifying of crystallizing process, just as water turns into the hexagonal lattices of ice. The thing—"

The bum chews the gum glumly and throws the wrapper on the ground. Michael picks it up and puts it in his pocket.

Peggy's voice says, 'You were bound to do it,' echoing Wecj's orders. Michael believes her because he knows what makes her suffer. Aware again of the cold wind in the night, Michael feels confused about where he is. He goes in search of light and finds a bar.

Wecj intended to publish Michael's work as his own, academic *droit de seigneur*. "You're only twenty," Wecj said.

"Mirror, mirror on the wall," Peggy said, "who's the genius of us all?"

He orders scotch. It's a bigger bar than he imagined, like a set for a cowboy movie, only in modern dress. The bartender at his end of the bar is a young woman with breasts displayed in a low-cut red blouse. She moves to the music. Michael wants to get drunk, stagger into the night to find a bed then fall into it like the vortex of Charybdis where he can drown alone without Tyler, his mother, Peggy – or Wecj.

When he orders the third scotch, the red-breasted woman says, "Honey, don't you think you've had enough?"

"Yes, I've had enough."

"You got someplace to get to?"

Michael blushes. The alcohol helps; she's thinking he is aroused by her nipple-edged breasts, which he is. He waves aside the messy moment with an open palm, pushing away any invitation to her bed because that's happened often enough. Women always want to look after him. It's the baby-blue eyes. He can't touch a woman now without feeling Peggy under his hand. She was ten the day he was born. They have the same birthday.

Michael walks out of the bar. Tyler was walking next to him on the bridge over the Charles in Cambridge, three miles from the university, a high wind Massachusetts day in late April. There was a stunning sun. Some sailboats sliced through shining water.

"Listen, don't let Wecj do it to you. The thing's not worth it."

Michael grabbed Tyler's forearm. "What're you talking about?"

"Everything."

The iron of Tyler's grip undoing Michael's was a surprise followed by shock as Tyler shoved him and ran to the edge of the stone bridge. Cars sped past. There had been Tyler's bent knee on the stone bridge ledge, his other leg taut and a lever pushing up, two hands on the ledge swinging over, a ballet-arc. Then he was gone. Michael was on the ground, where he'd been pushed. The back of his neck was stone, like the bridge, inclined upward, staring at the empty space that had contained Tyler. There were loud horns. He felt cold and raw, as if all his skin had been blown off in the April wind. He heard sirens. Someone arrived. Arms lifted him. His face was wet, but he couldn't feel his hands to wipe it away. That was then. Now, he knows precisely what to do – go home to Isle End.

It is almost dawn. The wind is rising. You can hardly feel it on the ground, but the treetops sway as if disconnected from their trunks, fine antennae to the air and light. It was a long train ride that goes only as far east as Port Wagner on Long Island. Michael steals a bike at the train station. It is five miles more from Port Wagner to Isle End. He feels numb as he approaches the Gottesman house. In the past, there had always been anticipation and relief in the curve of the road and the fractal tree branches, the straight line of the gravel driveway, and the big house whose windows were eyes, front door a smiling mouth saying 'welcome home'. Now he feels attached only to a stolen bicycle.

Like a stranger, he nears the side door. He knows where everything belongs except himself. There is a strange leftover smell from the kitchen window. Cabbage? He associates the smell with his stepmother sleeping upstairs beside Doctor Gottesman. In Michael's old bedroom sleeps their son.

He thinks of the doctor's office. He walks around the house like a thief – which he is – and rings the bell. He sees the light go on in the upstairs bedroom, hears the high-pitched sound of a little boy's voice. Michael rings the bell again and looks up. As the sky loses its stars, the office door opens.

Doctor Gottesman looks exactly as he did the last time Michael saw him, a year before at the conferring of degrees ceremony when his Ph.D. was awarded. They had not said much to each other then, and Michael can think of nothing to say now. The bathrobe Doctor Gottesman is wearing is new. His white hair is uncombed and his eyes are still filled with sleep. Doctor Gottesman takes hold of Michael's arm and leads him into the examining room. The hand feels strong on his arm and makes Michael feels suddenly weak throughout his body, as if all his energy has drained into his father. He almost falls.

To Doctor Gottesman, the young man looks like his first wife, whom he loved. Michael has her eyes and skin, but he has his father's narrow lips that always seemed to be demanding how and why.

"I'm sick."

"Let me take a look, then."

The room smells familiarly of alcohol, ointment and pills. Michael contrasts the office he shared with Peggy. There was a dusty mess of green chalkboard no one dared erase. Nor would anyone touch the papers, reports, and books for fear a scrap of work or a corner of equations on the board might later fit into place. Well, they could erase it now because they did. The equation is complete in Michael's mind, and in it the thing gleams like gold.

In winter, their university office smelled of nervous sweat in woolen sweaters and like stale air conditioning in the summer. It smelled of enclosure. The doctor's office is clean and antiseptic, whole and open, peaceful as always.

Doctor Gottesman directs Michael to lie down on the examination table. He leans over his son, pressing his stomach, then his abdomen.

"Does that hurt?" The doctor's voice is low, interested, and impersonal.

"It's sore."

"And there?"

"No."

"Sit up."

He taps Michael's back, then moves his hand lower, and using the side of his hand, sharply raps Michael's lower back twice on each side.

Michael sits up stiffly. "It's not kidneys."

"Can you keep anything down?"

"I can't remember."

"You need some tests. What else is the matter?"

"Matter," Michael whispers. His teeth begin chattering and he's trembling. He can't stop it because he isn't making it happen. The skin of his scalp is crawling in waves. He can't speak.

"You have fever."

With terrific effort, Michael speaks through clenched teeth. He hears a strange sound pass through his lips, as if someone else were groaning. His breath is short.

"Oh, Dad. I'm so scared."

"What are you scared of?" Doctor Gottesman takes the boy's arm to help him off the table then leads him down the hallway to his paneled office. He seats Michael in a leather chair facing the desk. He sits on the edge of the desk, close to the boy.

"I'm really scared."

"Yes. Of what?"

"The thing. I found the constant."

"Did you tell Wecj?"

"Why? He's not my father." The space between Michael's chair and the desk deepens and widens into a canyon.

Doctor Gottesman touches Michael's shoulder, feels him trembling, and puts his hand back on the edge of his desk.

"Refer me to a psychiatrist." Michael's hands have stopped shaking. A paralysis of some sort is taking over. His throat is tight. What time is it? What is time? "I stole a bike to get here from the train."

"It's light now. We'll go to the hospital in my car. Michael?"

That's it. That is the voice he'd come home for. It closes his eyes like fingertips, undresses him, puts him into bed and still speaks comfortingly as he falls into sleep. Michael's head becomes too heavy for his neck hold up. He bends over and holds it in his cold hands, leaning into his thighs, elbows pressing sharply.

"I want…" Michael begins, but he can't breathe.

Doctor Gottesman catches Michael as he falls. The doctor struggles to carry the young man to a couch. Doctor Gottesman calls his wife, then sits beside the boy, stroking the wet hair off Michael's forehead.

Michael hears a voice coming from the top of the well. He sees stars spiraling like firework pinwheels. He sinks again.

There is dark water at the bottom of the well, and he's beneath the water. He falls through rooms, but there is always a pillow beneath his cheek, and he can see with an interior eye that it is needle-pointed. The stitches are soothingly geometrical and handmade. Dark, wavy underwater currents lift and lower him. There is pain – a silver piercing.

Water has inundated Isle End. The flood has finally come. There were voices of women and children. When there is a field fire, water is strung along in buckets to save the harvest, but what can you do when water rushes in? Fire can't put out water.

"Michael, what did you say?"

Michael feels so sad. He moves his lips. It takes sound a long time to move through water. "The thing…"

"We're going to the hospital now."

"He doesn't hear you," Doctor Gottesman's wife speaks. "What is he whispering?"

What direction is the car going? The window glass is so cold against Michael's cheek.

"Therefore, it is clear…" The thing is so beautiful, gleaming. "Therefore, it is clear… 6.27×10^{36}…"

"It's all right… nearly there now… called ahead… expected."

Movement ceases. Which shell is the thing under? There is more silver piercing. Michael's lips are chapped and he is so heavy. He is sinking. Then many arms reach him, and he opens his wounded palms to them, borne off into their white embrace. Out of perfect hot darkness into cooling light something gleams, it shines. He can see.

Eulogy for Miss Eulalie

Mark Antony was wrong, I believe, when he said that the evil men do lives after them and the good is oft interred with their bones. Maybe it is that way for men. It is not for women – for Miss Eulalie. I am afraid we may forget her if we remember only what was good. I learned first from Miss Eulalie that what made a lasting image was contrast. Although she created in words and I in photographs, I learned that lesson best from her. I saw how she looked through the camera's eye to see what surrounded every object as clearly as the object itself. This is the way creators see; foreground and background are a *trompe d'oeil* of time. Space is a matter of shapes that curve about each other, of light and dark. Time provides the dimension of depth. Miss Eulalie talked about these things with me. Now that Miss Eulalie is fully in the Spirit at last, I have been asked to speak about her before all of you. When I was called to this honor, I at first felt the sadness we all share. Then I thought to myself that they have called me because of what they believe was the special bond between Miss Eulalie and me, between her people and my people, because we came from the same small town in Mississippi where she lived for nearly a century. You all know I've lived most of my nearly half-century up north and around the world, taking pictures. Miss Eulalie was a creature of place – her place – and I am not. Then I thought of all we have had in common, and I hit upon what I want to remember about Miss Eulalie with you today. I want to remember with you this good woman, this gentle and strong spirit. The best way to do this is to tell you about the meanest thing she ever did in her life. Yes, it is the sort of story Miss Eulalie would have liked to tell you herself, and of course she would have done it better than I can. I think if we all recall her voice, and keep the images sharply in focus, you will be able to imagine it is she telling a last story to all her friends and admirers.

All of us in that small town possess at least one Miss Eulalie story and we recognized them when she retold them in her books that made her famous – that made us famous. In later years, many of us who lived in that town had fun teasing the graduate students who came to do research for their very important doctorates. How many ladies pretended to be Miss Eulalie or her sister or her cousin? Yes, we had some fun!

But we all knew there was but one Miss Eulalie. When I was young, she was briefly taller than I, but very quickly it seemed she became that rumpled, wrinkled, blue-eyed face surrounded by untamable white curls. She gave to my family, as she did many other black folks, the only photographs of themselves they ever had. It was my Grandfather Aaron's most precious possession, his picture by Miss Eulalie. She gave me my first camera as a going-away present when I left for college in 1963. I never did know why Wellesley accepted me in those days, whether it was because I was a Miss Black Mississippi or because of the essay I'd written about Miss Eulalie, but I went up there with her blessing and her Eastman Kodak.

My freshman year roommate was the other person in this tale of the meanest thing Miss Eulalie ever did. Her name was Kathleen C. before she married a very rich New York man. Kathleen wasn't my roommate for very long, of course. She explained her moving out the first week as a matter of the room being too small, but we both understood that wasn't the real reason. I don't remember resenting the prejudice of Kathleen C. Everything up north at Wellesley was strange to me except that. It made me feel more at home.

It was possible to become friendly only at a distance with Kathleen. Over four years' time, I saw this was how it was for her with everyone else. She could not keep a friend of any color. Perhaps because I had met her first, I was one of the very few still speaking to her at the last. By that time, I knew many things about her. I knew about her friendlessness. I knew that her mother, a woman who looked like a Pekinese dog, was in and out of a New York mental hospital. I knew that both Kathleen and her mother, wealthy though they were, often shoplifted in New York department stores. I also knew that Kathleen C. wanted to be a writer; she had typed up all sorts of little notes to herself that she scotch-taped to the wall above her desk – things like 'character arises from plot'. I knew Kathleen could never understand anything she read. In our freshman year, it was I to whom she brought every poem or short story assigned in English for me to explain so that she could write her essay. Once she discovered I had grown up in the same town as Miss Eulalie and indeed knew the great Southern writer, Kathleen treated the information as if it were somehow a personal directive to her. That was how Kathleen C. was; the world was her oyster to steal the pearl from.

Almost two decades went by in which Miss Eulalie wrote more of her wonderful stories about us. They were made into plays sometimes, and sometimes into movies. Most of all, they were books people liked to read slowly to remind themselves about how time really moved. I traveled around the world taking pictures of wars, elections, 'movements' – and Miss Eulalie still managed to win more awards than I did.

It was at one of these award ceremonies last year when our three paths intersected, Miss Eulalie, Kathleen C., and I. It was in New York City where Kathleen and I lived, very differently. The Algonquin Hotel, an illustrious literary landmark, hosted the affair. Although Miss Eulalie had known the Algonquin *literati,* she had never been a member of their cynical set. Nevertheless, she was receiving a lifetime award at the charity dinner. She was seated at a long raised dais covered with a bright white cloth and many bouquets of flowers

like these here today. The people who had come to support the charity
– it was a three hundred dollar a plate dinner, more than annual in-
come some places in the world – sat at round tables before us in a
large, oak-paneled dining room. Miss Eulalie had asked that I be
seated beside her so I was at the dais as well. We shared a view of
the room, and she asked me what did I – professionally... see? I
looked at the floor-length gowns and tuxedos; some were worn by
people of my color. She nodded her white curly head at me. What
else, she asked. I saw waiters balancing heavy trays. I saw the musicians arrange themselves in their intimate, superior way. Then I saw
Kathleen C. seated at a table across the room. She was there without
her tall husband. She was staring straight at me. As our eyes met, she
sat up very straight and waved a small wave.

Miss Eulalie, you see, had noticed her staring at me, and Miss
Eulalie's curiosity was piqued. I explained quickly what I currently
knew about Kathleen, who had left a message on my phone machine
which I had unfortunately answered. I told Miss Eulalie that Kathleen, still now, after nearly twenty years of busy failure, was yet again
involved in her pursuit of personal money and fame.

"But she is rich," Miss Eulalie said.

"That's her husband's wealth. It's separate in her mind. Kathleen
once said, 'I don't keep a cook, I make my husband a hot gourmet
meal at whatever time he arrives home from the office, a trip, or the
squash court because I know there are plenty of women who would
be happy to make his meals for him.' Another time, she told me,

while she was basting a turkey, I recall, that she had not become famous while I had because my childhood had been so awful and hers so wonderful."

"We were poor," Miss Eulalie said, reciting the well-worn Southern phrase, "but we didn't know we were poor."

I explained to Miss Eulalie that Kathleen was not exactly motivated by charity to attend this dinner that honored her. Kathleen, true to form, had not written a story of her own whose blessing she wished to secure from Miss Eulalie. Kathleen had told me she had 'adapted' a novel of Miss Eulalie's into a stage play –a libretto, in fact – and she was working with a second composer and a third lyricist who were writing the songs. She was no better at keeping colleagues than she had been at keeping friends. Kathleen had run into legal problems when her agent – whose office was in one of the buildings owned by Kathleen's husband – told her that Miss Eulalie had to approve the use of her novel in this way. Miss Eulalie knew none of this, having been shielded from Kathleen, as from eager others, by her own lawyer, Mr. Marshall Burdett, who remembers with us here today.

Across the dining room, Kathleen C. motioned – lifted and shook slightly – a white box. Miss Eulalie looked at me. The musicians began to play. Several couples rose to dance. Kathleen approached us with the white box. I apologized to Miss Eulalie for my part in Kathleen's plot. I had suggested that Kathleen give her flowers, and I knew Miss Eulalie's favorites as you all see here – as a means of approaching the great lady with at least apparent generosity.

"Why?"

"Because Kathleen can never come up with an idea of her own. I felt sorry for her."

"Why?" Miss Eulalie persisted.

Cornered, I revealed the details of something that Kathleen had confided in me.

So Miss Eulalie accepted the gardenias and black-eyed susans from Kathleen and told her to send on her script home to Mississippi so she could read it. Kathleen, slim and elegant in a black gown and diamonds, thanked Miss Eulalie too many times.

Kathleen never pushed when she could shove. Though her script was a dismal washwater version of Miss Eulalie's novel, Miss Eulalie hardly had the heart to write this in her first letter to Kathleen, nor to add that the novel in question had already been successfully adapted in the Fifties into a Broadway play which enjoyed regular revivals around the country. Poor Kathleen was an embarrassment to a Wellesley education; she didn't even know how to research prior publication and production, or that she should. I was at home in Mississippi visiting Miss Eulalie for the last time because it was my cousin's child's graduation last June. I might as well have followed Miss Eulalie's letter back up to New York because Kathleen called me right away yet again, and I learned she had hired all sorts of expensive lawyers, whose offices were in buildings her husband owned, to secure the rights to Miss Eulalie's book despite Miss Eulalie's polite refusal. Miss Eulalie had a fight on her hands. It took a long Sunday to get Miss Eulalie 'tired out', as she'd say, but Kathleen C. finally tired Miss Eulalie out.

She wrote the second letter.

Kathleen sent me a copy of it because she couldn't understand it.

It was cruel.

It was very well written.

It was as unforgiving as it was unforgivable.

Miss Eulalie told Kathleen that she had absolutely no talent. She told her to quit writing, to quit writing to her, to quit bothering Mr. Marshall Burdett, and to quit stealing other people's stories if she wanted to get rich and famous on her own. Miss Eulalie added some choice remarks about the contrast between art and theft, indicating that Kathleen must have sorely misunderstood T.S. Eliot's remark that amateur poets borrow while professional poets steal. She wrote, "Tell the story of how your mother put a gun in her mouth and shot off the back of her head in a closet in an expensive condominium in Miami, Florida, on your birthday – and try to find someone you can work with long enough to set that to music."

That, I believe, is the meanest thing that Miss Eulalie ever did in her long, generous, good life. Maybe she knew it wouldn't stop Kathleen who was poor and didn't know she was poor.

Kathleen is writing yet another libretto of a still unsuspecting novelist's chief work. Fortunately, I am not acquainted with him.

It is difficult to say goodbye to Miss Eulalie. It is painful for me.

Maybe that is the real reason I have told you this particular story. I didn't like what she did – but I didn't like what Kathleen did, either. It came down to a choice. At least it was a clear contrast, a picture you could keep sharply in focus. Miss Eulalie gave me my first camera, her own. I pass along this final photo to you. I hope we all can now remember her well.

Flash Gordon

The house Professor Freeman Post Gordon owned was on a green lawn beside green woods on the water. He was known in Isle End as Flash Gordon. His housekeeper, Bette Awad, called him that behind his back, and the name stuck. She had confused the stories he told her children, Mambo and Mae, and their friends, primarily Richard Limb, with the Saturday morning television shows the children watched. Bette Awad's younger daughter, Mambo, was pretty and slim, black-haired like a kewpie doll. Her older sister, Mae, looked like a smudged version of Mambo; she was simple, perpetually six or seven years old, although her body at nineteen was a woman's and already tending to her mother's overweight. The house was a three-story greystone, unusual in Isle End. It had belonged to Flash Gordon's wife, Dorothy Potter Gordon. It was because Dorothy was an Ender that Flash Gordon had come out east every summer from Ohio where he taught medieval literature at a small college. When he had retired ten years before, they had returned to Isle End for good.

Dorothy Potter Gordon had died four years before this Sunday morning. Each day when Flash Gordon awakened, his first thought was of her. Then he checked his faculties. He was ninety. He knew the year. He knew the date. He felt the weather for damp or dry, cold or warm. This morning, he felt the spell of oppressive weather had been broken. There was something in the air that marked the end of summer and the beginning of things, understandable to a man who had lived a lifetime of September beginnings. It was not that. When the body begins to die, the mind begins to live. That was what awakened in Flash Gordon.

His was a life of habits, he acknowledged. One autumnal day in August does not mean it is October. He thought there was a day in each season that anticipated the season to come. This was such a day. Professor Gordon roused himself from the bed and slapped his feet on the wooden floor. He was still a tall man, over six feet, but he had lost an inch or two to old age, which, he supposed, science could explain. Perhaps because he had lasted longer than most of his generation, he had affection for science. It did not frighten him. Few things frightened Flash Gordon. There was little life could do to him that it had not already done. He was left with curiosity. He was partial to science in a personal way, too, because it had prolonged Dorothy's life and mind, and had given her a painless death. The century had not worked out according to the dire predictions of his peers who had seen the worst that human invention had to offer. Much of the past that had been blown away was chaff in the wind; this was Flash Gordon's point of view. He deserved his nickname more than Bette Awad could know.

It was a habit of his to awaken, stand, and do his exercises slowly. Then he took a shower, all the while discussing in a methodical, curious way some topic which had raised itself in his mind like a student's hand. Today, apparently, the topic was an evaluation of the twentieth century.

A story came to mind that he had read in some science magazine he subscribed to but rarely understood. He had also been reading the parables again, marveling at their eternal elusiveness, wondering what Jesus would have thought had he lived a long human life. The essay had been anthropological, about race. It was a suspect study, given the century. The essay said that four infants studied were kept in isolettes in a nursery ward. One was brown, one red, one white, and one yellow. Over the nose and mouth of each infant a gauze pad was placed. Three of the babies behaved similarly. They whimpered at first, but then they relaxed and breathed underneath the gauze. The white one resisted, screaming, flailing its arms and kicking its legs until the gauze was dislodged and it could breathe through its nose and suck its thumb.

Professor Gordon walked to his bathroom, undressing for his shower. He was shaking his head. The danger lies, he was thinking, in jumping to conclusions. Four infants was not demography. The story must have been apocryphal, a convenient foundation for the essayist's dubious thesis. Facts were hard, if not impossible, to come by. They were discreet, not the matter of probabilities relied upon in the essay. The four babies nicely summarized his century for him, but that uncovered nose and mouth had been far too bloodied to be called white. Probability appeared to be his second topic for the shower.

He liked the shower hard and the water hot. His stomach rumbled. It was pleasant to consider probability when the certainty of death was daily present. Seen this way, probability was one of the distancing functions of the mind, which could deceive itself about its ultimate dissolution. Even a good lie was a lie, confusing the century's progress with the ultimate end of days. He picked up the soft washcloth and carefully lifted his arm to soap the back of his neck and ears. Nothing betrays age as much as the spot on the tie and the scent of flesh. The problem with probability, which was the scientific fashion, was that it demanded immense perspective. The issue was scope. While some of their cyborg-instruments might have that perspective, the minds that received the widened sight didn't, and they distorted reception and reportage. Only time widened human perspective. It seemed such a sad fact that one gained perspective and insight only when the capacity to act declined by nature and was denied by society. Professor Gordon got out of the tub enclosure and sat on the toilet to dry his legs with a soft brown towel. The softness reminded him of Dorothy. She had been a scholar whose studies of Eleanor of Aquitaine sometimes seemed to him to be autobiographical evidence of reincarnation.

He dressed in a long-sleeved blue shirt, grey sweater, slacks, socks, and slippers, then descended the stairs. His thoughts moved from Dorothy, whom he always imagined now as sleeping on the pink satin ruffles in her coffin. He thought of his mother. She had died over a half century before. He was so much older than his mother had been when she died that he sometimes was able to imagine her as a girl. He went into the kitchen. Bette turned, like a barrel in a flowered housedress. His mother had always drunk morning tea from a flowered porcelain cup. He saw the white porcelain of her bones. He sat down at the square butcher block kitchen table, touching the knife furrows of decades, understanding again the silent power of medieval reliquaries for their devout owners.

"Good morning, Professor." Bette placed before him a bowl of Wheatena, a cup of tea, and small glass of prune juice.

He heard instead the name she called him by in her mind, *Flash Gordon*. He smiled, lifting the prune juice and toasting to her.

"I heard you up early this morning, near dawn when I had to bother about Mae. She had a nightmare, I believe. I can't think what could have gotten into that head, Professor. I'm sorry it woke you. Your hearing certainly is good. That's a way to look at it, I suppose."

Professor Gordon accepted the apology. He nodded. Speaking to the lonely woman unleashed floods of disconnected talk. He ate. He had always loved the taste of food, but he had never eaten very much. He must have learned strict habits in childhood. As he had gotten old, though, a new wrinkle had appeared. As he took in a meal, he felt it slowly suffusing his body with heat, as if he were personally, minutely, consuming the sun. It was a plain, homely ceremony that explained communion to him. A lifelong member of the Episcopal Church, he had never had the slightest feeling for his own religion. He had much preferred the fervors, both intellectual and sensual, of the Middle Ages, especially the twelfth century, that had built huge cathedrals to Venus in Mary's name, amen.

Bette was standing beside him at the table, watching him eat as if he were a child or blind. She appeared to him surrounded by noise, although at the moment she was herself quiet and still. A tiny television set was on that she was not exactly watching, but was alert to, like a cat to a bird. The sink disposal was strangling small wet garbage. In the living room, another television was on, watched, Professor Gordon presumed, by one of the daughters, probably Mae, as above him he heard the sound of a radio or stereo pulsing rock and roll music. The noise located Mambo in the house. The children's noise was associated in his mind with the mother. Then the kettle whistled irately on the gas stove, and the telephone rang. Mambo yelled down it was Richard Limb for her and she would get it. A car drove by outside too fast. Where was anyone speeding to in Isle End? He wouldn't have minded going deaf except for his music, but there didn't seem much probability of that if it hadn't happened by now.

"I'm like the Deacon's one horse shay, Mrs. Awad," he finally answered, startling her. She never expected him to speak any more than she would have one of the faces on Mount Rushmore. "—Which does not break down part by part, but only all at once, with a shiver and a thrill, gone from oak to immediate, immortal sawdust. Although it lasted precisely a century, I do not wish to worry you with the prospect of another ten years of looking after me."

"Oh, Professor, there's no call to be always talking of dying."

"It's all we have in common, Mrs. Awad." He meant humanity, but it was lost upon Bette, who felt insulted. Helpless, Professor Gordon rose, approved the breakfast, and began his daily round of the house.

It was another habit of his to take pleasure in the stone that made up the outer wall. It looked exactly like the human labor it had taken to build it. He rubbed one wrinkled hand against a chipped stone surface. His hands were brown-spotted, gnarled like bark, and blue-veined. He had watched them slowly change, but they still looked like strangers to him. He liked the chip in the stone. Dorothy had always worried over how to mend it. He touched its roughness like it was Braille. There were three things one could do with stone: build with it, look under it, and throw it. No, four – one could leave it alone. That had not occurred to him. It felt foreign to him, but he liked allowing for the alternative. One could throw stone at a building, too. That made five. He was amusing himself. No wonder true cathedrals were made of stone and the Taj Mahal of alabaster.

His constitutional led him to the water's edge. When he looked, he saw bubbles of clam breath pucker the sand. There was a nearly transparent quarter of the moon tipped up in the morning blue sky. It was *d* for *dernier*, the last quarter of the moon. That was a good detail to include in the last story he was writing, *The Dungeon Dream of Master Freeman.*

He thought of this last story. There was no window in the dungeon Master Freeman was thrown into by Lady Barbara's cuckolded husband, the Earl. Master Freeman would have to imagine the moon as he lay in the dirtied straw, dying. The moon would be dim, high over the waking town he had designed.

Professor Gordon walked the hundred fifty feet of beach property and no farther. He carefully turned at the line of stones he had directed Mambo to build for him when she was still a little girl. She kept it up every spring, neat as a New England fence maker. He knew how peculiar it was for him to walk off the property as he did, around the house, down to the water, and up the lawn to the asphalt road where Bette had planted daisies, measuring all these markers and never venturing beyond them. In old age he acted exactly as he pleased. There was no need for pretence to gain acceptance into a social group that had already ostracized him, thrown his bones out. The thought of leaving the property was unapproachable, as if, in accepting the certainty of his death, he had transferred its terror to the world beyond the road, beach, and trees on either side. He watched a thin string of cirrus clouds cross the moon. He could see the moon through it. It gave him a lovely feeling, like a lace fan moving across a beautiful woman's face. He felt constrained not to leave, just as Master Freeman was imprisoned in the dungeon.

Professor Gordon walked back toward the house, across the grass. He watched a cardinal fly up to the green copper gutter. It had not been cleaned in such a long time that leaves had turned to humus. Seeds carried by the wind or by birds had taken root. There were several tree seedlings growing out of the gutter, and there must have been insects for the cardinal to eat, because it was rooting busily. All kinds of ages had gone by and were coming. The difference between the magi and the man in the manger was the matter to be transmuted: men into gods.

He watched a few cars drive by. They waved. He waved back. Then it was time to turn and go to the music room which had been the dining room before he took all his meals in the kitchen. The dining room table, chairs, and china closet had been sold after Dorothy's death. She never would have parted with them. They had been replaced by a secondhand baby grand piano that could never stay in tune because it was so near the water. It was perpetually soggy. It suited him. If he stayed within the three middle octaves, it was endurable. Nature required these boundaries for pianos as well as man. His fingers, wrists, and elbows right up to his shoulder joints pained when he began to play. Each day he started with the scales he had hated, impatiently, as a boy. He remembered from childhood a scallop of lace spilling over the top of an upright piano. Now it reminded him of a Dali clock face. As he began his ritual at the piano, he waited for his hands to move until the blood came into them, replacing pain with warmth. Every function of every day was like that. Waking was a cacophony of screaming bulletins of aches; his body rebelled every day against waking. He exercised and showered to teach it – pain first, reward second. Every day his body was the boulder that Sisyphus, his mind, pushed up the rocky hill. He played the scales first then the songs he had always played for Dorothy. Then he rewarded himself with his opera study. He had finally arrived at *W* for Wagner. He was not happy about *Gotterdammerung* for its association with the Nazis, but he liked too much to hear the stories he knew intimately from years of study and teaching.

Mae sat beside him in a big armchair with an ottoman. She had her legs up comfortably. Every day she sat with him while he practiced. She had been leaving early since Wagner began, spending hours out of the house. Professor Gordon presumed Mae didn't care for Wagner. At times, during the scales, she asked him to repeat part of the fairy tales he told Mambo and Richard at night on the front porch. She knew these sections almost word for word. Like a small child, she corrected him if he forgot or improvised. Forcing his hands through the scales again, he looked at the girl. Her eyes were cast across the room, unfocused, to a loveseat where the Wagner librettos were stacked. Her hair was dark and curly like her younger sister's, but her nose was large and fleshy, and her were too round, like the dogs' of different dimensions in the fairytale. Her hands had six fingers each. The small finger was sub-divided into one normal-sized and an additional stubby part, complete to knuckle and nail. Mae was altogether like that sixth finger – poorly formed, unnecessary, but meaning to be helpful and eager to stay close. Blood was beginning to run into his hands. They began to feel strong. What was to be done about Mae and the other outcasts of a world that prized beauty and power beyond all else? Why should the cast outs, not the wild flowers, the weeds like Mae, not wish to rule in hell rather than serve in heaven that had created hell?

Mae shifted in her chair, awaiting Professor Gordon's selection of his tune. At times, Mae called him Flash Gordon as her mother did, but to his face, because she did not understand the mockery and certainly felt none. He even liked to hear Mae call him by that name, even though the medieval knight had managed to survive only in ridiculous costumes in erector-set ships that couldn't possibly stay afloat, let alone aloft. What was beyond aloft? There was no word for it. He would have to think about that, but now to the music.

He felt warm and good, but fatigue was beginning to round his shoulders and drag at his eyelids. The haunting, haunted lyrics of *Begin the Beguine* sang in his mind as he played and danced with Dorothy once more. From C to a B flat bridge to A flat and G7 and back to the tonic, the Cole Porter song moved from heartbreak to transcendence, affirming the music's power to restore a lost love. Then he thought of Act Two in *Tristan*. Oh, what Wagner could have done if had not been a Hun!

"Oh susse Nacht! Ew-ge Nacht! Hehr erhab'ne Liebes-Nacht!"
he sang.

Mae clapped her hands, then looked to the window where the stereo cabinet was. Professor Gordon nodded.

"Yes," he apologized. "It's time for *Gotterdammerung* now."

Mae jumped up and ran outside, banging the kitchen screen door, as if called. What power propelled her, he wondered, as he walked across the room to put two records on at a time. Adams had written about the Virgin and the Dynamo as the power sources for the medieval and industrial ages. He had that perspective when he was only sixty-three. The first record dropped. Professor Gordon shut his eyes. No unique power source, not the dynamo, could explain life now – not coal, steam, even oil, or the inside of an atom. No. The sad Norns? The Fates? Macbeth's witches? No. Flash Gordon's ship… nuts and bolts on a coffee can; ridiculous. Remember that sailboat, its wooden hull and red and white sails? Dorothy was listening. Her white curls fitted around her small ears. Remember sailing east to Apple Island? Kant, Freud, Darwin and Frazier lifted the lines that held her to the dock. Off she was sailing and we were all in our dinghies, following: regatta of the mind, Dorothy. Mind: there's the power. Locate the priests and you'll find the myth. Falling to sleep was drifting into another language. "Dammert der Tag? Oder leuchtet die Lohe? Getrubt trugt sich mein Blick."

Wagner always put him to sleep.

"Were you dreaming, Professor?" Mambo awakened him with

her hand upon his shoulder.

He opened his eyes. The girl's face was perfect, heart-shaped, cream skin now tanned, and wide set large brown eyes with the slightest oriental tilt that made her look exotic in daylight, at night, otherworldly. Her neck was narrow and her shoulders thin, bird-like. She was too small-framed ever to be a great beauty, but her delicacy, inexplicable as it was given her thick mother, made Professor Gordon wonder. Her hair fell from her crown in Nile waves. She was not of Isle End. Mambo would become, he believed, a woman who would torment poets, like young Richard Limb.

"Were you dreaming?" Mambo repeated. "Your eyes were moving under the lids really fast. I've never seen anything like it."

"Yes."

"Can you remember your dreams? I can, every night. Every night, when I go to bed, the dreams I had the night before come back, speeded up – instant replay. I always recognize them."

"I remember only two things, Mambo. Great pieces of sycamore bark were covering the lawn like leaves, and a dwarf with Mae's face was entertaining the Earl's loutish vassals. "

"What do you think it means? Lunch is ready, by the way."

"What?"

"My dream."

"Did you tell me your dream, Mambo?"

Her grimace told him she had, while he had been woolgathering. She was impatient.

"I just did. I opened a clam shell, but on the inside it was an oyster, all bluey-white." She shuddered intentionally. "I hate oysters. I hate the way they look, and I hate the way they feel in your mouth."

Mambo offered Professor Gordon her hand. He stood, feeling her strength, warmth, smoothness. His own hand, by comparison, felt dry and looked like a veined, old, brown leaf.

"Clams don't make pearls," he said.

"It can't be worth it." Mambo wrinkled up her pretty face. "Do you understand it?" she asked again.

He saw the lunch her mother had prepared, and was pleased. She had put a blue-checked tablecloth on the table and placed a cold glass, beaded with water, of buttermilk on a dark blue plate beside a larger white bowl of tomato fish chowder. His stomach growled. Mambo looked impatient. How alike his stomach and the girl were, he thought.

"I was admiring your mother's work," he apologized. "Your dream... an explanation; unlike Joseph, I have no gift for interpretation. What do you think?" He realized she was bursting with her own idea.

"I think it's Richard Limb... the oyster part."

"But you like him, don't you? He's crazy about you."

Bette had entered the kitchen as her daughter spoke. Mambo ignored her mother.

"It's that creepy eye."

"That's not kind, Mambo. He can't help his eyes any more than I can help being so old."

"You're not creepy. You don't make me sad."

"Well, you can have any boy in Isle End you want, and Port Wagner, too, for that matter."

Bette presented Mambo with lunch.

"Oh, he doesn't hang around here to be with me. I hope you don't think that! It's the Professor he's crazy about, and Castle Culwish and all."

"Cul-wich," Professor Gordon corrected. He knew her error had been nastiness.

Mambo looked darkly at her plate, chewing ruminatively. "I'll tell you frankly, Professor, it's not the sort of story I'd tell. There's got to more sex in it if you expect it to sell."

Professor Gordon swallowed buttermilk, lolling it over his tongue slowly, as one must with yogurt and juice nectars. He heard Mambo, but distantly.

"Sell?"

"Oh, okay, romance, then." Mambo reacted to a pursing of Bette's lips that sent up fine webby lines around the housekeeper's mouth. Professor Gordon found it threatening, like the wrinkles around a volcano.

"Come now, the blue weddings at the end of *The Conquest of the West Country* should more than satisfy you."

"There were too many blue-painted legs and arms, and you couldn't tell who was doing what to who. Orgies aren't any good."

Turning from the sink, her mother snapped, "What do you know about orgies?"

"You only know the Master Builder in that one, and he doesn't even take part. He only watches. Richard thinks he's a prig."

Bette slammed a cupboard door. "A what?"

"He loves Lady Barbara," Professor Gordon protested.

"Oh, sleeping in a burning tree doesn't thrill me, I'm sorry. I can't buy that."

"How would you tell the story?"

Mambo leaned toward him, both arms on the table, talking and chewing excitedly. "Now, see, I'm glad you asked, because Richard and I have been talking about this a lot. I've got to keep him talking, you know, or he gets disgusting. I think you've got a basically good story going, but you've slowed it down with too many descriptions. A lot of writers do that, and I'll tell you, it only interests teachers, not the people who buy books in supermarkets. Stick with the Earl. He's the one. You've got to concentrate where the muscle is; that gets people hot, so in the blue-people orgy, mixing it up with the conquered Welsh women – it's okay to slaughter off the men – follow the Earl, not the Builder, and really let him loose. Then when you bring in that dippy Lady Barbara in the next story—"

"*The Hidden Meadow of the Sun*," Professor Gordon offered.

"Whatever – then when you bring her in, all white-handed and musical, and looking at the world through the stained glass windows the Builder puts in for her, then you understand right away why the

Earl can't get too excited over her and has to go out and firestorm the rest of the country. Frankly, though…" Mambo took another bite and chewed, thinking aloud. "…if I had my way, I'd get rid of her and the Builder altogether and put some girl the Earl kidnapped in the tower – you know, some red-headed Welsh girl who resisted him and who was keeping a prisoner, waiting—"

"Like the morsels a spider keeps in a corner of a web?"

"That's it, Professor! Stir up the blood. You could use the Builder then, if you had to, to help Tower Girl escape with his workmen through the hidden passages he'd designed, just because he was crazy about her, too, although the Builder, of course, wouldn't stand a chance with her. The Earl would catch them in the escape and rape her right then and there! You'd have 'em in the aisles. Then when the Earl had the Builder tortured in the last story, his love torment – not being able to have Tower Girl because she was too much woman for him – makes some sense."

"A Master Builder and a lusty peasant, is it?"

"That's my suggestions, Professor," Mambo said, hearing his tone. "You can take it or leave it. I'm only passing it along. Anyway," she stood abruptly, "I'm going to leave Isle End soon and write my own stories for movies… or television, where you can make something of it." Then she was out the back door, slamming the screen, calling for Mae.

"My girl has a lot of ambition."

A loud buzzing sounded from the basement.

"Yes."

"That's the dryer. I have laundry to get. I want to get your cleaning today, too. I hope she doesn't bother you any. She thinks the world of you."

"Thank you, Mrs. Awad. I think I will get to work on my stories now."

He rose and walked with some effort. He felt full, and after lunch, always heavier and slower. The red swellings under his eyes felt hot. He walked to the latter-day parlor which was now his study. Bookcases lined one wall and flanked the fireplace. The sun was high above the house, and the room was filled with undirected light. The wide bay window over the porch was open and a crisp breeze blew through the white silk gauze. His large desk was set in front of the bay window, in imperial position like King Canute ordering the ocean to cease. On the desk were stacks of books, a neatened pile of papers, and Dorothy's porcelain cachepot filled with pencils and real ink pens. The day's mail was placed beside his papers, the Culwich stories. On the floor by the fireplace was an antique foot scraper, now very dull brass, in the shape of a cat. His eyes always fell to it, as to a pet, in memory of all the cats that Dorothy, he, and the boys had reared from kittens. Sarastro had been all yellow, and when the sun hit him, he turned to shimmering gold. Huck has been a wandering tom, always returning wet, ripped, and hungry. Macavity had slept on books in the library back in Ohio. This was Professor Gordon's favorite room in the house, and the part of the day he liked best. He took the letters from the desk and sat in the large leather wing chair that stood before the bookcases and faced the window. He lifted his feet onto the small, unicorn-needlepoint footstool that a student of Dorothy's had sewn for her. One letter came from Ohio, from a recently retired young colleague who was seventy-five.

Professor Gordon sighed. What a wealth of opinions he had found the world filled with, and so much fool's gold! Perhaps he had held some opinions from time to time himself. He thought of Mambo at the lunch table. He had listened for nearly ninety years and fortunately could not remember all he had heard. The listener was a mirror. Under the surface, he held his own opinions, but he had not felt they were worth voicing. It seemed idiotic to add to the noise. What he had said, or published, had been done to survive, as all the worst things that people were apt to do were. Professor Gordon looked up from the letter and watched the wind blow. The little girl's opinions of his stories might be right; he didn't care. That wasn't the point of them. How viscous the mind becomes in the afternoon. The only fact he could remember from helping his younger son study chemistry was that at first heating sulfur results in liquid, and further heating renders it viscous. In any case, it was foul-smelling. He had made these stories. They lay on his desk, and the wind could easily and carelessly blow them away... and his room full of books, the fireplace, the dull bronze cat – this stone house altogether, his world, and the Earth...

He thought of a human head, the Earth, spinning, wet, hot and cold, with small brain centers of various capacities. Science had accepted a prime moment of creation and measured it in degrees of radiation. Adrift in it? Was adrift the word after afloat, aloft? In space, adrift? 'Give me that patience, patience that I need now,' he heard Lear's echo.

Frankly, Mambo, he believed in before and after, eternal attempts, infinite patience not sex alone, which was why the cathedrals had decayed. Virgin worship had been displaced by regained Venus worship that had gone into underground streams and surfaced elsewhere in time and space, perhaps like new fountaining universes themselves. Even the ungrateful, aggressive masculine assaults of Israel and Greece could not stanch her flow, nor close the spaciousness of her wide, loving arms: not sex alone.

There was something beyond the flailing arms of galaxies that embraced all, as a fountain draws water down to geyser it up. The presence of whatever this embrace was he felt undeniable. Letter in hand, feet on foot stool, bags under his old eyes, wind blowing through the curtain – he wrote his little stories because he didn't know how else to show he held onto this whatness of it all. Moliere must have written the letter in his hand, as the character of some petty fool on his cosmic stage. All his life, Professor Gordon had listened to hear if anything would speak other than the monkey chatter of other human minds, filling up the voice with their noise. The wonder was that there was no void, and saying that was worthwhile.

Not all sex, frank little Mambo, who was discovering one part, and like her species, believing it to be the whole. The elephant touched by blind men presents a universe of different realities. Where, on the elephant, could they touch the mind, the secretly growing part that was always pushing out, making more room, expanding as had the universe at creation? Elasticity: his skin, like parchment, had lost its elasticity, but not his mind. He had lost just about everything but his mind. That was where Lear had come from.

Professor Gordon examined the return addresses on the two other letters. He saw one was from the old publisher who was going to print his stories. Professor Gordon got out of the chair. He wanted to work on *The Dungeon Dream*. He wanted to get that moon he'd seen in the morning into the dying Builder's mind. He picked up the last chapter from the desk, fixing his attention on it, and at the same time realized that the third letter had been from the boy, Richard Limb, with his clouded eye. His mind, though viscous, was slowly slippery and could be in more than one place at one time. The letter made him curious, but he held the last chapter in his hand, and his life of discipline held him to it. *The Dungeon Dream-Tale the Fourth* was the most difficult to write because it contained the least action. The Builder was confined in the winter-cold, dark and foul-smelling – that was why they called it dung – dungeon. What was left to an imprisoned man but memories, and what was less interesting to the young?

Professor Gordon had to keep the chains chafing the Master Builder, and hungry rats biting pieces of his loosening flesh away.

This was as far along in the story as he had come. He knew he was avoiding the Builder's thoughts about his impending death. Professor Gordon looked up from the paper and with the black fountain pen he held in his right hand, idly tapped out two large blots of black ink. They sank into the dark red blotter in stains that stretched out in fine webs like a strange map. He could not imagine the Builder would welcome his death any more than he did his own. It was terrible loneliness for Lady Barbara that the Builder felt, not pain. Pain had one value: it made death a relief. There was a chemical that Professor Gordon had read about, in the brain. It was activated by mortal pain: endorphin. Unlike nature, the Earl had no merciful traits.

Professor Gordon gazed out the window and began to see what he was looking at when he heard gravel being harshly stirred. Mambo was running up the driveway. She looked horrified. Some adolescent catastrophe was coming upon him. It would come when it would come, some-thing would be done, and it would resolve itself one way or another. That was the feeling of the Builder in the dungeon, he realized. Adrift, was it? He was chained within walls no one knew the solidity of so well as their builder. Pip in the ocean went mad. When it came upon the mind too young, it drowned, but now, so late in life and with everything accomplished including sacrifice, the Master Builder felt buoyed. That's where the veil on the moon must come in, the cloud moving away, removing the veil. Mambo burst into the room.

"He's going to kill himself! Because his father—!"

Her face was almost purple, and she was painfully out of breath. Bette and Mae didn't appear. Professor Gordon looked at the girl dumbly.

"Richard's—" she gasped, "at the Wagner Estate. He's gonna jump. He won't listen to me. You're the only one who matters to him."

"Call the police and tell them."

"No, no!" Mambo stamped. "Sirens – he'll jump! Maybe he has already!"

Professor Gordon stood, leaving the opened fountain pen on his scattered notes. He felt frustration at not having time to write down the conclusion. "That is why the police must be notified, to call the Coast Guard. Go to the telephone and speak slowly."

He looked down at his slippers and out the window at the road fronting the lawn. His eye went to the marker of daisies. Mambo returned.

"Where are your mother and the car?"

"I don't know. Not in the driveway. We've got to go!"

"Then we must walk."

"I'll ride on ahead on my bike and tell him you're coming. I told him you'd come. I told him to wait for you."

He watched her spray gravel on either side of the bicycle as she raced up the driveway, and he walked beside the grooved path. As he passed the bush of white daisies, he noticed that just beyond them a mound of tiger lilies leaned toward the sun. He had not known they were there. The sight of them now drew him past the point of no return, and the passage was painless. Things and places he had not seen in years were wonderful to him. A vegetable stand was at the end of the road. It was a live sculpture of bulging yellow squash – who would think the delicate orange blossom could transform into something so sturdy and comical? – beside dusty beets, little straw baskets of raspberries and blueberries dark as night sky, and heads of white cauliflower sticking out of their stiff green collars, like figures in Rembrandt's *Night Watch*. Professor Gordon began to feel dizzy.

Stopping then, he felt his legs tremble and stood waiting for their rebellion to pass. On the table-flat surface of a tall Queen Anne's lace flower, he saw a daddy longlegs spider with only two legs left, set at diagonals, balancing the mutilated creature. Its body was mottled, dusty brown. Having lost six legs, it hobbled across the flower face and managed to swing its way from the top and down the hard green stalk of the weed. With no mental fanfare, he felt the spider's fine-tipped deliberate motion, inexorable, and felt his own leg-trembling, easy distraction. Everything called his eyes and his ears away. The effort was to move to the goal of the desperate boy. The wind blew, flickering birch leaves moved yellow and green under the blue sky, and he heard the subdued daytime rasp of crickets. Reminded, he resumed his pace.

It was a very long walk. Professor Gordon's legs had begun to feel light. He kept walking, although he didn't think he would be able to reach the Wagner Estate. He came upon a field that stretched open to others, neat green rows and irrigation wheels at the ends of the rows spraying as far as he could see. Workers bent over the rows, picking beans or berries he could not see. A car approached behind him. He turned and saw it was a police car. Its red light was flashing, but it was not wailing. He recognized the driver, but not the other officer with him.

"Professor?" the driver asked with concern.

"I'm going to the Wagner Estate for the Limb boy."

"We got the call." The officer helped Professor Gordon into the car. They sped away, the field of migrant workers turning into a blur. He was distracted by incessant radio static, a voice that with attention took on meaning.

"Do you listen to that all the time?"

"Sure."

The other policeman pointed to a dilapidated frame farmhouse they were passing. "There she is. We have a domestic disturbance there to get back to."

"This one's the emergency. Surprised to see you left your place, Professor."

"I know the boy, or rather, he knows me. Do you know his parents?"

The two officers exchanged a look; the driver spoke. "That was his house we just passed. Father's an alcoholic, beats the wife… the kid's real smart, y'know, the poetic type. He's got that eye. He's supposed to go away to college next month on a scholarship."

They were at the estate. Professor Gordon saw Mambo's bicycle lying on the wide marble steps of the old ruin. He had not seen the building in many years. Its broken windows looked like gouged eyes, the front door a gaping mouth – what a human skull must look like an-other months in the earth. Still, the blue-sky sun was shining down on the white stone building, and the surf beside the palisade-like mansion sounded like a loud heartbeat. The policemen stepped outside quickly and moved their heads as if to sense the boy's location. Then they remembered Professor Gordon, and the driver opened the door and helped him out. He felt heavy in the young man's grip, as Dorothy had felt in his arms on their wedding night, substantial and willing.

"We can stop him, sir, but maybe you can save him."

"What?"

"Out on the terrace, right over the damn ledge."

The three of them walked through the empty mansion. Professor Gordon followed at a distance that lengthened. He traveled through viscous atmosphere in time clocked by spider legs. He was very tired. He heard the sound of Dorothy's breath in his ear and the pounding of her heart against his chest. There was a clasping. The pounding was the ocean, but Dorothy was also present, drawn into the dream or up from his unconscious with a tingling effort. His legs were falling asleep. He could see Dorothy's young face, all asmile for him. He was so glad to see her! The ballroom floor upon which he walked was a pattern of black and white marble squares. Above him were chandeliers of moving crystals, but many of the crystals were gone. There were empty spaces, like the two legs left to the spider. Children gave the crystals as love tokens before they left for Apple Island. Professor Gordon saw Mambo silhouetted against the outdoor sun where French door should have been. Her arms were spread dramatically, forming a small *t*. He knew that Richard Limb had given her a crystal. He saw the two policemen move past the girl, at her silent nod, toward the terrace. They blocked his vision of the boy. Mambo came near.

"I must see the cellar."

"He said his father's been at Mae."

"Take me down to the cellar," Professor Gordon repeated.

Afraid, Mambo turned from him toward the terrace.

"You must escape now, my Lady. My men will take you away on the ship we have hidden below the cliff, and you will be safe with them. I must stay here to give you time."

"He's been raping my sister!" Mambo screamed.

"Richard!" Professor Gordon shouted suddenly. Mambo jumped back as if he had hit her. It was an order. "Richard, come here! I need you!"

The two policemen, at this moment, were kneeling at the edge of the terrace, talking quietly to the boy whose legs were already over and who held on sitting up, leaning over, with only the fingertips of his right hand touching the ledge for balance. The uniformed men started at the sound of Professor Gordon's command. One cursed under his breath, grabbing at Richard to keep him from falling forward. The old man's voice had the opposite effect on the boy. He held still and listened.

"Richard! Come here now! Come here!" Professor Gordon repeated.

Richard Limb swung his legs effortlessly away from the precipice, ignoring the hungry looks of the two policemen. He ran into the ballroom. When he saw Professor Gordon, he stopped. There was awful understanding on his young face.

"Oh, no." To Mambo, furious, he said, "We're not worth it!"

"You must take care of her for me."

The policemen entered the ballroom and watched silently

"I know I can trust you, Richard."

"I tried to write to you about—" Richard silenced himself.

"You must lead me to the cellar." Professor Gordon's voice had changed timbre.

"There's nothing there."

"Why did you want to die?"

Richard walked to the old man and put his arm around his shoulder. They were the same height. Richard looked at the two policemen, requesting their aid. Mambo stood aside, utterly mystified.

"It doesn't matter."

The three young men walked toward the cellar doorway.

"Yes, it does."

"I won't do it again."

"You must not. You must protect the lady."

They were walking down stairs. The air changed to mildew damp with the smell of salt water in it – old, wet wood. It was dark, getting darker. He looked at the face beside him – high forehead, locks of fair hair, the occluded eye, like a pearl in a darkening light. He reached out his nearly weightless hand to touch the boy's face, and Richard shut his eye. He touched its soft lid.

"You will see," Professor Gordon said.

The two policemen shifted uncomfortably.

Richard said, "Leave us alone," but they already had.

It was completely dark. The boy was beside him. The sea beat against the walls. It was the ocean. It was his heart.

"I am sorry." Richard was crying. "Thank you."

He took Professor Gordon's hand and held it.

"You have promised me." Professor Gordon felt the cat's soft fur move against his hand. He wondered which one it was.

"I promise you." Richard heard footsteps rushing about, above.

Professor Gordon heard purring near his ear. Her ship was safely away. The boy would keep her safe. He had his promise. A veil of cloud passed over the white moon above Castle Culwich. The veil cleared the moon. It was a perfect pearl in the sky. He reached toward it, and it drew him upward. He floated. He rose above... aloft... adrift... "Away," he breathed. *Away.*

Richard Limb heard his rattling breath.

Away and away.

The American Wing

My older sister, who was a genius, knew the name of the virus right away when Zeff – that's what my parents called Doctor Zeff Fessenden – explained on the phone to my mother why he'd be late to the dinner party for which they had, at that moment, been expecting him to arrive. The dining room table was set with the blue-and-white Wedgwood, silver, and my dead grandmother's Waterford; only the tall candles needed lighting. The other couple my parents expected were also a bit late, but they could be having trouble with their car, a thirteen-year-old Toyota. My mother had been sipping a drink my father had made for her just before Zeff's call. The three of us – my father in the rocking chair by the fireplace, me on the couch, and seventeen year old Lily in the big chair with the ottoman on the other side of the fireplace – all became audience to my mother's side of the conversation, trying to make sense of what she was saying.

Her smile changed to a frown as she listened to Zeff. "I read about that in *The Sciences*. How did it get here?" my mother asked.

Daddy, Lily, and I exchanged looks. It wasn't enough to go on. It was like Lily and Daddy doing the Sunday Times crossword every week; there weren't enough letters yet.

"Will she let you take blood? Was he in Arizona?"

Zeff was chief doctor of epidemics for the National Institute of Health in our county.

Lily asked, "Hanta virus?" and my mother nodded.

When she got off the phone, she told us that Zeff was in the middle of an investigation of the death of a twenty-two-year-old Long Island student who had died of the fatal disease which, up until that moment, had not been found outside of the Southwest.

The doorbell rang and the Campbells arrived. I made myself scarce because they had not brought their kids, so I was unwelcome at the grownup dinner table although Lily, who would be eighteen in two months, was. She had been accepted early at Guess What U. and had won about a million national awards already. I played Sega in the basement, watched some TV upstairs in the den and listened in at the kitchen door. Everyone except me was sitting at the dinner table when the doorbell rang again. It was Zeff, and everyone wanted to hear his news. Later no one minded when I sat next to my mother on the couch and Zeff answered more questions about the disease. What he said scared me because there was no cure and he was in our living room. My mother got up and asked me to help her clear the first round of dishes in the kitchen.

Lily and I were having winter break from school that week in February. My parents had decided to take Friday off from work so they could have the dinner party on Thursday night and we could go to a museum together on Friday. My father worked for the IRS, my mother was an emergency room nurse. That was how she had met Zeff, when he was interning.

The next morning I slept late and so did Lily. I was awakened by the sound of the computer printer in my parents' bedroom because it was against the wall my bed was on. My mother must have been printing out a letter because when I walked downstairs in my pajamas, I heard her reading it aloud to my father in the den. It was a letter about Lily who should have been valedictorian of her high school class. This had been an enormous deal in our house in October when ranking was announced in the high school; Lily had come home crying because Donald Jacobsen, whom she'd been in class with since kindergarten and was always miles ahead of, had come up to her to smirk, "I'm Number One, and you're Number Two." My parents found out that it was the school's grade weighting and ranking policy that had dropped Lily behind Donald. My parents had gone to speak to the high school principal who admitted the district policy was to blame; he wrote a letter about Lily to all the colleges she applied to so they knew she was secretly the valedictorian while publicly, Donald would remain the named one because if everyone found out, all the grades and ranks would have to be redone and it would be a big mess. My parents agreed to that deal with the understanding that the new superintendent and principal would look into changing the policy so I could go on playing the double bass in the orchestra without it hurting my future rank, like a younger sister had any chance in the world of ever being in the top ten.

What had happened was that earlier in the week of the dinner party and the hanta virus arrival on Long Island, my parents had received a letter from the superintendent of schools and the high school principal saying they had changed the weighting-ranking policy. My mother's letter, the one she was reading to my father in the den, was her reaction to that letter. Now she wanted them to reconsider and let Lily be co-valedictorian with Donald.

"But we agreed not to ask for anything more," my father advised.

I was standing in the kitchen doorway out of their sight.

"You make me sound like the fisherman's wife in the fairy tale, always wanting more, but it's just not fair. It's still not fair."

They argued for a long time without raising their voices.

"You always turn things into an attack on you," my mother sighed.

"You're accusing me—"

"I feel like Lady Macbeth married to Hamlet."

"Look, if you feel it isn't enough, it isn't enough."

"I just don't want to be alone in this. I've been alone before and it caused a death."

"Let's not go into all that again."

"It wasn't your body."

"I know I've failed you. This is always about my failure."

I heard her stand up. I got ready to disappear.

"I don't want to do this anymore. I'm the biggest failure I know, not you."

Then my mother did what she always did when she was unhappy. She went to bed and stayed there all Friday day and night.

My father bought Chinese food for Lily and me for dinner. She and I watched Tonya Harding's skate lace crisis and Nancy Kerrigan win the silver. She was one tenth behind the sixteen year old Russian girl who wore an awful outfit with pink fuzz around her arms. I thought of Lily and Donald, but I didn't say anything. There was no talking in our house that day or night.

The next morning, Saturday, I was in no rush to get out of bed. Doctor Zeff had been on television the night before, in front of a zillion microphones and cameras, talking very slowly about the hanta virus and the Center for Disease Control. It was weird to see someone on television who had just been in our living room, except my mother's cousin who had been on television a lot because he was a big shot county politician and also my best friend from camp's father who was on *Saturday Night Live*. I slept over several times at her apartment in the city so I had seen people I knew on television before. Also, my mother's older brother, my Uncle Martin, had won a Nobel Prize for chemistry, and I'd seen him on TV, too. The hanta virus scared me.

I heard voices from downstairs, though, and peeked into the hall to see if Lily's bedroom door was open. It wasn't, so that meant that my parents were talking. Even through the floor, I could tell the talk was different from the argument. I went to the top of the stairs and listened. My mother sounded okay. My father was asking her if she wanted to go to the museum and she said sure. Then she must have seen my big Goofy slippers Lily had given me for Christmas at the top of the stairs and she called out to me. Did I want to go to the museum? I said sure, too.

I woke Lily and told her what we were doing. We did shifts of breakfast and quick showers. By the time I was dressed and downstairs ready to eat, my father was coming up the front walk. My mother said he had gone out to cash money. He was carrying a little box from the jewelry store and he handed it to her when he came through the door. It was a gold ring with a woman on it, like an entirely gold cameo. One of the woman's breasts was exposed. She was looking off to the right. It was her left breast. My mother was very happy with the ring. She showed it to Lily and me, let me try it on and fussed over it all day.

We went into the city by train. It was very cold and windy, but sunny. We got a cab from Penn Station to the Metropolitan Museum on Fifth Avenue. My parents and Lily had certain ideas about where they wanted to look in the museum. They were huge urns filled with yellow forsythia in the Great Hall. It'd just snowed for the fourteenth time that winter the night before so it was nice to see the flowers.

Lily wanted to see the new Dégas exhibit which was landscapes.

I got lost in the nineteenth century European paintings. My mother found me and made me look at a Van Gogh of blue irises against a white wall. She also dragged me through an early Renaissance Spanish court-yard which looked down like balconies over a court with a fountain where some younger kids were throwing coins. But she got wrapped up looking at some round tapestry deal and roped my father into looking at it with her. My mother was always very keen on tapestries because "women did them." My father liked the Rodin room the best because the black statues had enormous feet and hands. He was very funny about the body parts and made me laugh although my big toe was starting to hurt in my sneakers. Lily was having a conversation with my mother when we got to the Egyptian hallway on the way to the Temple of Dendur. Lily was talking to her about the cowrie shell necklace-collar belonging to this Queen Meroe and whispered in their secret conversation voice how the cowrie shell was shaped like the crotch of the Rodin dancer who held up her foot backwards like the Russian ice skater had, 'exposing her Volvo'. I didn't ask.

My mother remembered me as we entered the Temple of Dendur room and faced the big, black, flat pool. "We had to fish you out of that when you were three. Do you remember?"

I didn't. My father, who had been our guide through the museum, referring to the map he had made a beeline for back in the Great Hall, led us to the back of the Temple where you would never believe there was a double glass doorway to the new American Wing.

The first thing I saw were baseball cards from the early 1900s. I was wearing my new Braves jacket. Little League tryouts were the first weekend in March, and my time card was already up on the refrigerator at home. There was a long hall of grandfather clocks my father liked, and then this whole, like, greenhouse room built on the outside of the museum. You could see the windows and doors where the museum had stopped before this tremendous build-on.

"It's like the museum is making a display of itself, its old wall," I described, and my mother looked at me with my favorite face – the one that said I'd surprised her.

There was an upstairs and a downstairs to this huge solarium. You could see outside the wall of glass into Central Park where someone was rollerblading in the freezing cold, and several New Yorkers were jogging past hills and boulders covered with old and new snow. I sat down on a cedar bench between two potted trees while my parents and Lily oo-ed and ah-ed over Tiffany stained glass doors, old engraved silver, and lots of sculptures. I watched a little boy in a wheelchair being pushed around by his mother. He had cerebral palsy, I thought, but he wasn't drooling. He wore a striped T-shirt, matching pants, and little sneakers, much too little for the rest of his body size. He liked the statue of the Indian and the one of the three standing bears. I shut my eyes and the sunlight from outside the window came through my lids like it did through the glass. At lunch my mother had asked, "What did you see that you think you'll remember?" I said the painting of the woman in a long Victorian dress leaning over to look at a painting in the Metropolitan Museum when it was on Four-teenth Street. My father was surprised the museum had originally been on Fourteenth Street. Sitting in the solarium, I opened my eyes and looked at the little boy in the wheelchair again. We were all like things in a museum to be looked at.

My mother said we had only one more place to go in the American Wing so we could go home on an off-peak time train. It was a wall-papered eighteenth century area. My mother read and commented that the wallpaper was a year older than the Constitution. I was look-ing for a portrait of Mercy Otis Warren because I had to write a term paper on her and had been taking notes since November. As it turned out, there was no Mercy Warren, but Lily led me into one of those little rooms they create – you go through a narrow doorway but are barred from entering some dead person's living room from the sev-enteen hundreds where they have backlit the windows and put in meadow scenes behind the paned glass. This small dark room had two green wing chairs on either side of the big fireplace, a card table with real old cards on it, and side-board furniture with candles and candelabra, pictures on the wallpapered wall.

I found my mother sitting on a bench outside the room.

"Pretty good, hmm, honey?"

I sat down next to her and took from my sneaker a pebble that had been hurting my big toe for a long time.

"We could live in there. Then we wouldn't have the long trip home."

"It does look like our living room, doesn't it?" my mother said.

I leaned against her soft parka and shut my eyes. She put her arm around me. I pictured the dinner party right in that museum room. I could see Zeff sitting in the left-hand green wing chair.

On the train, Lily sat next to my mother, and I sat next to my father. After Jamaica Station, when a noisy bunch of teenagers got out, I asked, "Maybe one day our den with the forty-five inch TV will be a room in the museum. What do you think?"

His eyes widened and he smiled. "Tell that to your mother when we get home. Maybe it'll make her happy. In fact, tell her right away at the diner."

He knew the diner was my favorite place to go for supper. After a day of trains, lunch at the museum, and cabs, we were going out for supper, too.

"She's happy already, Daddy."

I looked to where Lily was sitting with her eyes closed. My mother saw me and smiled. The window of the train was backlit by sunset. A blur of bare trees and attached houses rushed by. We were heading east. I locked my hands together at the palms and flapped just one.

"Get it, Daddy?" I said. "The American wing."

The End of the Cold War

The rain hit the house as Cara stood snug by the front bay window, holding a china mug of English tea. During Christmas break from college, her freshman son Daniel had explained that snow was ten inches to every one of rain, so on this Wednesday night in late January, Cara imagined the deep drifts this storm could have been. Most of her knowledge came secondhand from her children, husband, or news media. Her older son, a senior, had left her a book from a sociology course. It was an indictment of her life. "Upper middle class and upper class women are parasites." If this rain had been snow, the only sound would have been the whine of the wind as it curved around the north corner of the house. The rain was now a waterfall cascading down the gutters of the home on several acres in a Gatsby-country suburb. On either side of the house, beyond the walkway lights, were trees and obscured neighbors' homes. Cara sipped the hot tea. It smelled like history: nineteenth century England and India or anywhere the sun did not set on the British Empire. She stood in her dining room while her husband Roger was asleep in the den with the Times open on his lap to the Metro section. Roger had every reason to be exhausted. He was the chief American executive of a Japanese corporation, one of whose widescreens was producing the low hum of entertainment that had lulled him. He had only that day returned from Japan, and jet lag had caught up. They should have lived in Westchester, north of Manhattan, along with his colleagues. The Japanese were conservative about this, as they were about many things. When they came for dinner, Cara was not welcome at her own table. She stayed in the kitchen with the gourmet food she had prepared and supervised the waiter she had to employ. Cara had insisted on living on northern Long Island because her mother's family still lived in Queens, one of New York's four outer boroughs.

The tea comforted. She reached into the moment as into a cashmere sweater, one arm at a time. Then she felt a thud; tea shuddered in her mug. The electricity went out. Roger did not awaken; she did not call him.

Cara groped her way to the entryway closet and found a large flashlight. She pulled on a lined raincoat and secured the hood, foregoing an umbrella in the mauling storm. Outdoors, she panned the heavy flashlight around the front lawn. Bare oaks and maples swayed and creaked, but the rhododendrons were submissively flat-leafed; it was warm for January. Cara saw, in the blown beams of light, a jumbo jet, its back third broken away – a mangled giant, marked with a colossal red stripe, ripped open, huge on the hillside.

She smelled metal, feared fire and explosion – then Roger was beside her. "Call nine-one-one!" she ordered, and he disappeared. Time telescoped; helicopters roared above the storm. There were sirens everywhere, red and blue flashing lights, voices on bullhorns, electric wires hissing at the rain. Roger returned and they climbed the slope of land from their property to its edge where the hulk lay broken. Cara knelt. She opened her coat to hold a baby girl against her chest and looked for the mother. She lost sight of Roger. Later, she saw him on the TV news, one link in a human chain lifting bleeding passengers from the wreckage until rescue workers, arriving in battalions, called them off and replaced them. She saw the body of a baby girl taken from a central casting's country club woman's arms, not recognizing herself but hearing the police officer telling her to go home and avoid the hot wires on the road. Cara wondered that such gentility could happen in a world where the sky really did fall.

Reporters speculated that since there had been no sound of engines, no explosion, nor smell of fuel, the jet had glided into the crash because its tanks were empty. Seventy-three died.

A week went by before Cara left Roger a brief note and fled.

She crossed the country the slowest way she could imagine, by Greyhound to Los Angeles. Cara didn't want to get anywhere fast. She wanted to melt like the Witch of the West at the end of Oz. She listened for hundreds of miles to conversation among passengers and various drivers about improved profits in 1989 and union demands for increased wages.

"SOB Fred Currey's out to bust the union," a red-faced passenger barked.

"Bust *this*!" The driver lifted a hand off the wheel and made a fist.

She made no effort to hide her whereabouts from the family; she knew they could easily trace her credit card use. She even called, the second week in LA, and told Roger that she was visiting the only living relative of her father's generation, his sister, her Aunt Maria. Cara had never been to Los Angeles before. She had never liked business trips with Roger that left her alone in hotel rooms in cities and countries where she was at most a stranger to herself. Raising the boys had freed her for two decades; she and Roger were relieved by periodic separations. Except for sex, had they ever been close? As she had traveled across the country in the bus, going south and then west, the weather had brightened and warmed. She had left the cold behind in New York; in Los Angeles, it was early summer.

Aunt Maria had never been more than an address Cara knew and a television image now a generation outdated, but she welcomed her niece as if she'd been expecting her. She lived in a suburb where the streets were lined with palm trees. Cara thought they looked like prehistoric, giant spiders. Aunt Maria, though, looked excellent for her upcoming ninetieth birthday. She lived in a white stucco house with a Mexican housekeeper in her seventies. They clearly had been together for decades.

Aunt Maria looked like Cara's father and was just as brusque. "Why are you here?" Before Cara could answer, she continued, "You look like your mother. All her girls did – tall, very pretty, good hair… I heard you all did well."

"I was told you didn't want to hear about any of us."

"Oh, that was your mother talking. Jealous and possessive, she was." Aunt Maria leaned on Lupe's arm as they ushered Cara into a sunken living room. White baskets of garish china flowers and giant lamps of the same unglazed Italian porcelain crowded table tops.

"*Capodimonte*," Aunt Maria accented proudly. "Aren't they beautiful? I'm a member of the TV *Home Buying Show*, and when they have them on, I buy them all. I've talked to most of the hosts by now. Do you get the *Home Buying Show* on Long Island?"

"I really don't know."

They sat on brocade furniture. Lupe brought iced tea and joined them.

"Not your cuppa? Want something stronger?" Aunt Maria offered.

Neither waiting for a reply or order, Lupe took the sweating glass out of Cara's hand and soon replaced it with several fingers of scotch.

Aunt Maria was blunt again. "I saw on TV an entire airplane fell in your front yard. They said that Columbians smuggled in drug-filled condoms in their intestines."

"Colombians," Lupe indicted in her low, unaccented voice.

"Right in your front yard," Aunt Maria repeated.

Cara downed half the glass of Scotch. "The baby girl was decap-itated."

"You'll stay right here," Aunt Maria ordered.

Despite having avoided the skies, Cara slept as if jet-lagged for days. She had never suffered from depression before but had heard the definition. She did not feel sad. Aunt Maria did not trouble her with doctors, or at all. When Cara managed to come to the dinner table, she was fed. Aunt Maria and Lupe went on with their lives not as if Cara had never appeared, but as if she were a new particularly fragile piece of *capodimonte*. Cara found out things about her father's family she had never realized she wanted to know.

"The Melitos are all still in Brooklyn, above or below ground. I am the black sheep of the family – the one who got away."

"The one who got away," Cara echoed.

Aunt Maria asked Cara about her sons.

"Roger is the older one, named for his father. Roger Allen Revere the fourth. Daniel is named for my father."

"How do you get Daniel from Dominick? How could they knock down the Berlin Wall? Now we'll never be rid of those goddamn Re-publicans."

Cara, who had begun dressing for the day again, paused at the buttons on her blouse. She had become familiar with Aunt Maria's abrupt shifts of thought but couldn't help worrying about mini-strokes. Lupe, however, looked as unperturbed as Cara was about having the two older women in her room as she put on clothes. In the same spirit as her aunt's segue-less conversation, Cara said, "I've never been unhappy, Aunt Maria. The 60's and 70's passed me by. I married Roger, who my mother said was such a feather in my cap, and the boys were born."

"What happened in the 80's?" Aunt Maria asked. "What do you do?"

Cara displayed her outfit for approval.

"What d'you care what anyone thinks? You've lost too much weight."

Cara laughed and followed her outside into the small garden where oranges, lemons, and limes grew. The sun was bright and hot. Lupe did not join them.

"I run." Cara lifted the gold chain around her neck and showed her aunt its thick golden '50' charm. "I won this for running fifty miles."

"In the marathon? I thought that was twenty-five miles."

"No, it's twenty-six, but I run at a track at the public high school. Daniel goes to a private day school. Every day, I run at least ten miles. Even in rain or snow. I do a lot of fund-raising for his school."

"At a track. You run in a circle ten miles every day?"

"And once a year, fifty miles. Oh, I can see how it sounds to you. You left Brooklyn and the family in the 20's and went to Chicago."

Aunt Maria was not about to let Cara retell her life story. "Yes, I sang and danced in prohibition saloons. By the time the 30's arrived, I headed west for the Busby Berkeley movies." She would have repeated the story Cara now knew by heart if Lupe had not come out-doors with breakfast and taken over.

"You were part of a petal in an overhead shot."

Aunt Maria took her story back. "My best times were the 40's, dancing with all the GIs in the USO canteens. The sitcom in the early 60's bought this house, thank God, because before that, I lived like a gypsy. I never saved money. I can tell you about—"

"…All the LA real estate you could have bought when it was sand lots, but—" Lupe interrupted.

"…Bing Crosby and Bob Hope were buying it up when we all thought they were 'on the road'," Aunt Maria triumphantly com-pleted her sentence.

Cara had been in California for three months. Nelson Mandela was released from prison. Roger called weekly and sent dozens of yellow roses for the same Valentine's Day that the space probe Voy-ager 1 took photos of the entire solar system and the Iranians issued their *fatwa* against a novelist. The day after, baseball owners locked out players. Both sons had written. On March eighteenth in Boston, thieves stole thirteen paintings from the Isabella Stewart Gardner Museum. Cara touched the unread copy of *Satanic Verses* Aunt Maria displayed with the *capodimonte* on the coffee table.

"I don't feel guilty," Cara picked up the book then put it down.

"Neither should Rushdie. Oh, you mean about your freedom? That's because it's not about you. You came here to bury me." Her wrinkled face stretched into a grin. "You're in my will now."

Cara stood up from the brocade couch. "It's always someone else's will. I was crazy to come here."

"You were dying, too."

"You're too mean to die."

When Aunt Maria smiled, Cara saw the Cheshire Cat in a spidery palm tree. Her heart thudded.

"*Cara mia*," Aunt Maria pressed, "When you appeared at our front door, I told Lupe that in LA, the Angel of Death comes dressed like a New Yorker."

Cara picked up an empty porcelain vase and walked to the entry where she smashed it on the Mexican tiles. Then she knelt and picked up the broken pieces carelessly, cutting herself several times before Lupe rushed in at Aunt Maria's yell. Even diluted by the flood of tears, Cara saw that her blood was redder than the shattered *capodimonte* roses.

Aunt Maria died in her sleep before Easter. Lupe was distraught so Cara managed the funeral, burying her golden '50' necklace in her aunt's coffin. In a month's time, Cara stood in the May morning back in the Long Island dining room, sipping another cup of tea. Through the Japanese corporation's power wielded by Roger, the process had begun to expedite Cara's adoption of a little girl from the horrible, newly-opened orphanages of Romania. She would name the child Maria Romano, and Lupe would become her *abuela*. She remembered a son's math text: no more circles; tangents. Cara was not surprised that her pleasure in that cup of tea was short-lived.

August of the same year, Roger traveled to Kuwait and was trapped with other foreigners to be used by Saddam Hussein as human shields to protect strategic Iraqi installations in the incipient first Gulf War. When international outcry and pressure secured the hostages' release in December, 1990, Roger returned to Long Island's hilly north shore, where instead of the wintry gusts off the Sound, all he could smell was the stink of the oil fields he couldn't escape in his nightmares that awakened Cara, who comforted him. He asked her to accompany him on long walks. He talked about freedom and phase changes in matter. She talked about Aunt Maria and Busby Berkeley. Roger told Cara that under their feet rose and fell the terminal moraine of the last receding glacier. Roger returned to work, but it was not business as usual. It was the last decade of the twentieth century, the end of the Cold War.

Throw the Bones of Your Mother Behind You

I looked up from my drawing into the blinding sunlight but could not see more than the shapes of the bodies speaking above me. Among the dark, deep voices speaking rapid Greek was a familiar woman's voice also speaking in that strange language. Beside me in the trench dug ten feet into this archeological earth was another member of the Brit team, a girl in her twenties named Juliet. She and I got on only civilly because she was a London type and I was a Scot she nicknamed 'Burr', more I think for my temperament than my thick accent. I was sketching Juliet's dig, out of which were emerging large decorated jars and something which, at this stage, looked like a shelf. Juliet could speak Greek.

Juliet translated, "You are raising the dead. We go to pick tomatoes and see the bright light before the sun rises over – solid bodies – carrying shields above their heads."

"Who are they?" I asked Juliet.

She shushed me, threatening me with the brush. An official-sounding voice spoke above us then.

"The police," Juliet said. "Agreement with Athens not to disturb the quality of life on Santorini—"

"Tell that to the dogs who own this island—"

Then again came the voice that could silence me – that of the American professor who was the director of the expedition; Irene Demas. She had my left upper incisor in her shorts pocket.

"We will of course do all we can," Juliet translated, "to stop – to eliminate – this disturbance."

A peasant's deep voice interrupted.

"What? You must stop the digging! My vines will not grow under ghost – under the feet of ghosts!"

Irene's voice replied, drifting down out of the murderous sunlight like a cool breeze. Juliet translated. "We will watch. Then we will try to understand and—"

Juliet turned to me, at a loss for words. "It's like 'make amends', I think, but I don't know the expression. There are lambs in it."

The police official spoke in English. "You will stop the excavation?"

"I will watch, myself, tonight," Irene repeated. "This is your island. We are guests in your home."

The official spoke in Greek too guttural and rapid for Juliet to translate, but she had no trouble with the farmer's thanks. "*Efkaristo, sas efkaristo poli.*"

I climbed out of the trench, letting Irene see I was there, but keep-ing a distance as the group leaders joined her. My Brit boss and a professor from Athens, assistant to the big shot for whose idea Irene had been able to marshal the necessary money, were there. What we were doing in the 60's on the Cycladic island of Santorini/Thera, in the best and hottest summer of my life, was digging up Atlantis.

In the *Timaeus*, Plato told the story about a divinely circular island in the western ocean. 'But afterwards there occurred violent earth-quakes and floods; and in a single day and night of misfortune…the island of Atlantis… disappeared in the depths of the sea.' The big shot from Athens was a seismologist who had reported his findings of a sixteenth century b.c.e. volcanic eruption on an island sixty miles north of Crete. The tidal wave from the Atlantis eruption had been anywhere from two hundred to seven hundred fifty feet high when it hit land all around the eastern Mediterranean. The Athenian also the-orized that the Atlantis explosion explained the lowering and rising of coastal water described in Exodus. In other words, the eruption at Atlantis, five times stronger than Krakatoa, was the apocalyptic event of the ancient world, remembered in the fundamental stories of West-ern civilization. When Atlantis exploded, drowning surrounding is-lands and most of Crete, it became the first place where the end of the world began.

Greece was in the midst of a *coup d'etat*, and the big shot in Athens hadn't been able to get funding to prove his theories. Enter

Professor Irene Demas, now with my incisor in her pocket. The States were having their own imperial problems in Southeast Asia at the time, but from what I understood, the war only made the country richer. As a most junior assistant professor in scientific illustration at Cambridge, I was ignorant of all these matters until, tempted by a fantastic summer salary, I was impressed into service to join the Cambridge part of the archeological expedition. There were land folk from the States, Britain, and Athens, and American sea folk with astonishing tech equipment from the Woods Hole Oceanographic Labs, ships and seismologists, scientists, archeologists, mythologists, photographers, and lucky me, the one with the colored pens and pencils and the expensive paper all paid for by the Americans.

In the afternoon, when work had been called off, Professor Demas located me deep within one of the cliff caves where I daily went during lunch-siesta, pretending to sketch though actually sipping bottled water and sleeping on a colorful woolen throw rug.

Irene pronounced, "I need a bodyguard for tonight."

She was nearly fifty then; I was twenty-seven. She was five feet tall and thin as a boy except for the curve of her hips and braless breasts. She wore her brown hair braided and coiled like a crown, grey at the temples like her eyes. I had seen Irene Demas calm wild dogs with words in their language, which only possibly was Greek. She had seen me with the three Athens toughs who'd tried to mug her on our first night in Greece before the expedition had flown over to Thera.

Then, I only knew her by sight from the plane trip from London. We arrived at Athens midday and had spent most of the afternoon getting to our hotel and reaffirming arrangements for the flight to the island. I was glad to let the grownups take care of all of it and to try my luck with Juliet. The result was that I slept alone the rest of that afternoon into evening and was nudged awake by my roommate, John, an overeducated fellow from Cornwall eager for companionship for dinner in a strange city. The July night felt as hot as noon in Britain. The crowded, noisy, modern streets were a great disappointment. Like any first-time tourist to Athens, I imagined I would be traveling back in time as well as space. John and I ate oily food and drank mentholated wine. I abandoned John to his own devices, which convinced him I was a stereotypically antisocial Scot.

I became lost trying to regain the hotel. Thankfully, some American college kids approached me with their instant coffee camaraderie and correctly directed me. I remember alleys of whitewashed stone, stinks of strange foods and organic fluids, and above all, the nauseating sounds of an alien language closing in on me. People leaned out windows. Everywhere there were second story balconies like those unearthed on Thera.

I saw a tiny woman in a long khaki skirt and white blouse walking ahead of me. I recognized her as the American professor. She had a sweater or shawl tied around her shoulders. Self-possessed, holding her sack close to her body. I heard footsteps behind me. Three boys ran past me, waving me off with threats I didn't need to translate.

They blocked her path. She spoke to them in cool-toned Greek, and maybe she would have handled them as ably as she did the dogs on Thera, but I saw one of them lean in for her sack.

I expected to fight, so fists and some feet, and a whistle! That was Irene, blowing a piercing whistle. I got two of the three down quickly. I was sweating, and it was so hot, I drank the blood in my mouth like water. I faced the third teddy boy. I hit him easily; his hands were up in protest, not in fists.

"*Parakalo, parakalo,*" he kept crying. The three of them lay on the stone street. People were above, calling out, some curses, some cheers that Irene translated later, and there was Irene, holding a small shiny revolver in her left hand. She knelt and picked up a bloody tooth from the ground – my incisor. She wrapped it in a tissue from her sack and placed my tooth in her skirt pocket. Shortly after, at a hospital emergency clinic, she offered it to a dental surgeon. She told me she had retrieved it for this reason, but I already knew better about that woman. She had an eye for bones.

At noon in the grey Theran cave, I protested, "You don't need a bodyguard against Minoan ghosts or anything else."

"The report of a woman alone would not be believed. The men chose you to accompany me."

"Should I believe you?"

For the first time, Irene looked surprised by something I said.

"There are fifty underlings you could have sent on this errand," I added.

"I'm what they call in the States a micromanager. My husband, of course, called it something else." She wore no ring and noticed my glance.

"Where, tonight?"

From her shorts pocket she took a hand-drawn – my work – map of the site and pointed to a group of huge, flat blocks believed to have been part of a palace wall or, possibly, temple altar stones. I nodded in compliance. At the cave entrance, which was a natural opening in the rock cliff that over centuries had been bricked into formal arches appropriate to the religious rituals performed inside the caves, the professor paused, almost as if she could see herself from my perspective, doubly framed by archway and the sunshine outside. Her face was completely hidden in shadow, her form haloed in white light. Only her voice reached me.

"I was disappointed in Athens." Her American accent sounded sheared, like a sheep. "I was disappointed in myself," she repeated, "to find your violence erotic, but it was the men who chose you because you act more like a bodyguard than an academic." Her unease managed to make it sound like an insult as much as a compliment. Then the space she had darkly filled was empty and became a brilliant doorway.

That cadmium white light stirs, in my memory, into the matte black spinel of that Theran night. It felt different from other nights when I had swum in the caldera and lain on a quay, cooled by the *meltami*, the summer wind that never stopped blowing. Then I had been with others and scorned their romantic tales of history and myth.

That night, I climbed alone to the Akroteri ruins. I carried a large torch, but it hardly penetrated a darkness that seemed to go back in time as well as space, so I gave up and turned out the light, laying down my sleep rug on one of the wide stones. I had never seen the stars so close. I heard the professor approach before I saw the beam of light from her torch.

I had resolved not to make conversation. Apparently, Irene had made the same decision, so we sat or walked about mutely, separately, for several hours. I watched the zodiac slowly move across the sky. I won. Irene broke the silence. She sounded like an oracle.

"*Kalliste* – most beautiful – was its first name, this island. Jason interpreted the dream of one of his Argonauts on their return with the Golden Fleece. Jason told Euphemus to throw a handful of earth into the sea. *Kalliste* grew up out of the water from that toss. Euphemus' descendents settled on Lemnos then Sparta, and finally Theras came here. The island is named Thera for him."

"Where did Santorini come from?"

"For Saint Irene of Thessalonika, patron saint of the island." Irene moved into the crossed beams of our torches which lighted her from below. "How did you learn to fight like that?"

"Until a month ago, I was illustrating pig dissections and teaching a class frequented as often by anatomy students from the med school as by art students. I learned to fight by being hit, which is why I left."

Silence. She won. I said, "You believe the Athenian's theory that Deukalion's flood was the tsunami of the Atlantis eruption?"

"We're trying to excavate the truth."

"I don't understand the archeological quest."

In the torchlight all I could see was her lower torso and the blunted outline of the stones. The sky was close, the ground still gave off heat, and the wind never stopped blowing.

"Neither did my husband. He was more interested in holding on to the future than the past. He married one of his students – your age, I should guess. The dentist in Athens was amazed by your eyes."

"Did he think I was a *Nea Kameni* vampire?"

Irene laughed.

"That's a yes. Do you have children?"

"They're teenagers at camp in their father's custody for the summer. I wondered if your eyes were like a cat's and would reflect light in the dark."

My eyes were a hazel so pale they looked yellow, rimmed by remnant RNA for dark brown pigment in three rings. My mutant iris looked like Plato's map of Atlantis before the eruption. I returned to steadier ground. "There was the flood, a dove and land. Deukalion went ashore to pray for the restoration of humanity. 'Throw the bones of your mother behind you,' the oracle said. Deukalion—"

"…And his wife, Pyrrha," Irene added.

"…And his wife, Pyrrha, decoded that it meant to throw stones over their shoulders. Where the stones landed, men and women sprang up."

At that moment, at Irene's ankles I saw two black snakes appear.

She felt them and looked down. "These are harmless." To my horror, she bent over and took one up in each hand. The crescent moon had risen high enough so that it looked like a crown on her coiled hair, her bare neck as white as the moon. Untrustworthy, recreated memory! The torchlight stayed on the ground, but that is how I remember it, Irene standing like a Minoan goddess, snakes in hand, winding around her bare arms.

We must have slept. I know this: we came awake in the dark with the sense of dawn near. The stars were occluded by cloud. The cow horns of the moon must have passed overhead to the other side of the mountaintop. I was lying on the rug and Irene was close beside me. I turned. I couldn't see her face.

"*Parakalo.* Please."

"*Ne,*" she whispered. "Yes."

Euripedes wrote, 'And in the very surge and breaking of the flood, the wave threw up a bull, a fierce and monstrous thing, and with his bellowing the land was wholly filled.' The bellowing noise was the earthquake. It was the dogs barking that night on Thera. It was my blood pounding in my ears. I saw lightning like no lightning I had seen before, many-branched like a giant tree. It lasted too long, on and on for seconds, for minutes. This lightning was the same that lighted Jason the way through the volcanic cloud's darkness to neighboring Anaphe. The eruption ejected ten cubic miles of island up into sky so far it was seen and recorded in China. The exhausted island sank thirteen hundred feet into the sea, forming the beautiful caldera bay where now *varcas* bobbed in the light, which also came. A brief shower, like a mist, cooled us. Cloud rose off the water, rolling like waves above the waves. It rose up the mountainside over the sleeping white houses tucked into the cliff face, and it floated in the fields which our mountaintop view spread below us. She was small, peaceful on my chest.

"This is where the end of the world began," she breathed, was quiet for more heartbeats then startled, sitting up. "Look!"

I followed the line of her snake-bare arm. In a distant field, the cloud-like mists assumed human shapes, and the sky was lighted from beneath the rim of the wine dark sea. Silver light was turning gold. Then in a trumpet-like silence, out of the bronzing Mediterranean the sun rose, huge, whole and round, pink, then as if reddening with arousal.

"It's the mist!" Irene laughed. "It's the mist!"

The climbing sun rayed down and through the earth-clouds, making the uppermost layer gleam like blinding metal shields. Irene stood up, her back to me, watching the quickening *meltami* move the mist like a battalion. I found her long skirt on the altar stone. I dug out my lost tooth from her pocket and threw it away behind me.

The mist explanation satisfied the locals. It was the professor's deference to them that mollified the peasants; I doubt anyone in authority had ever treated them with respect before, back to the time before the Minoans had escaped the flood. Where had they all gone, the thirty thousand or more *Kalliæteans* whose skeletons were never found but one? One human skeleton and one piglet were left alone on all Thera before the end of the world. Who warned them? How did they know? Where did they go? The researchers debated these questions endlessly throughout August as the frantic excavating continued against a deadline and the daily threat of the mercurial moods of Greek generals and xenophobes.

I knew. The high priestess had saved her people, directing them to sail to their ports in Phoenicia and Spain, to outposts as far north as England. Millennia later, when the Romans finally came, we fled again farther north and west. Those snakes Saint Patrick banished from Eire and the standing stones in the Orkneys where I summered as a boy were not the first end of the world at all. The beautiful island thrown into the ancient sea had generated immortal waves.

Viktor

Viktor was in honors English, a junior accelerated among competitive seniors. He was pale and his fair hair was almost white. His skull was sharply visible under taut skin; in class, Dale was able to keep the seniors from calling him 'Yorick'. He was the brightest and would easily have led the group if it were not for his temper. He snapped at the boys and dismissed with a snort anything said by a girl. Dale had spoken to him after class, but when she had assigned excerpts of Yeats' translation of Dante's *Inferno*, Viktor read the entire *Commedia* on his own and wrote a long story that identified her as Beatrice. She encouraged Viktor to publish it in the school literary magazine she supervised. The boy began writing to her.

In February, 1975, Margaret Thatcher was elected leader of the Tory Party. In March, the Eagles' *Best of My Love* reached number one. It was Dale's fifth year of teaching at a high school with a view of the lower NYC skyline the Twin Towers had dominated for two years. In April, the Khmer Rouge began the regime that resulted in the death of three million, and Bill Gates founded Microsoft in Albuquerque, New Mexico. After Viktor's letters turned up in her mailbox, or he tossed one onto her desk at the start of other classes, Dale answered as promptly as she could. She became afraid the boy might misunderstand, and she had no respect for teachers who liked playing Pied Piper.

She went to Viktor's guidance counselor, Florence, who was on the phone. Dale had about four minutes to report her concern about Viktor before the bell rang. Florence hung up, rubbing her forehead.

"What brings you—?" Florence asked.

"Viktor Heinz is too attached to me."

"It's spring and you're pretty."

"He acts out – in an honors class."

Florence found the boy's folder. "Highest IQ in the junior class. Youngest of three, older sisters your age. Family moved here in ninth grade."

"His oldest sister named her twins after him, which he finds disgusting. They moved because his father's inn out in Montauk burned down. Viktor was there alone and feels responsible."

"He was alone?"

"He wrote that his mother chose the morning after the fire to tell him she'd been married before, that the sisters are half-sisters. For marrying twice, his mother is a 'fallen woman'."

"I'll speak to him tomorrow the latest."

The bell had sounded and 2400 students were crowding halls built for 1800.

"The call of the wild," Dale said. "I'll be late to class."

At the end of the next day, Dale sat at her desk reading essays. Viktor appeared.

"You weren't in class," Dale said.

"I was in Guidance," he said.

"We all need guidance."

"She only talked about the SATs. I ought to do fine," Viktor paused, "as long as *Wrut* is in charge."

Viktor wore a blue sport shirt and chinos. He folded his hands on the student desk. "Mrs. Citron did inform me about your concern about my behavior and I want to allay any future fears you may have in that regard. It is cruel of me to overreact in the classroom situation, although there have been occasions when, after my story appeared, everyone attacked in a vicious, merciless way, not realizing it was the imaginary outcropping of my structural philosophy. I will not upset you in class in the future. I hope you will accept my apology."

"Of course."

"I think it is perhaps time to clarify those references I made in my last letter to, as I said, my structural philosophy." On that Thursday afternoon in April, Viktor hid his face inside his folded arms and gave a ninety minute monologue about three forces in his personality. *Wrut* drove him, *Marauder* threatened, and *Danla* protected him. "They combine into *Pilgrim Walker*." Viktor lifted his head.

"I'd like to write a philosophical play about the three factions of my character. It could incorporate all the ideas and questions I have been exploring lately. I have also neglected to tell you of a strange dream I had about you last Wednesday. I was attending a mass at the church I used to attend when I was feeling pious. The celebration of the Eucharist was just beginning. I don't know if you are familiar with Catholic doctrine, but when I was small, the altar boys used to ring a bell three times during the Consecration. Each time you were supposed to beat your right hand upon your heart. In recent years, the ritual had largely disappeared. In my dream, there were two nuns in red and black habits seated behind me to the right. They were both beating their right hands across their hearts. Just then, the usher beyond their pew looked at me and smiled, nodding his head at the two as if pointing out their senility. When I again observed them, one was holding the other's hand and hacking against her wrist with her free hand, drawing blood. In the midst of the Communion, I made my way to the rear of the church and began to ascend the staircase leading to the second floor balcony and the organ. As I was about halfway up, I met you coming down."

"That's a dream about me?"

A custodian pushed a wheeled garbage pail into the room. Dale greeted him, placed the essays into her briefcase, and put on her jacket.

"We'll be out of your way in a sec, Anthony."

Viktor walked with Dale down the hall to the parking lot exit.

"There's one other thing I must tell you," Viktor said. "I'm afraid what I have to say may end everything, but," he whispered, "I abuse myself twenty times a day. Sometimes forty."

Dale's hand was on the door. "I've got to get home now, Viktor. My husband will be waiting."

Viktor took a step back and let her go.

She called in sick the next day to read student essays. A school secretary called to say a bouquet of flowers from Viktor's mother had arrived for her, and a colleague would drop them off on his way home. On Monday, an eleven page letter from Viktor waited in her mailbox. Dale read it to Florence in Guidance.

"*I encountered a practical and clear-cut thought in Dostoevsky's* Crime and Punishment, *who, as you know, in the course of narration slips in small remarks and comments on topics such as pathological dreams or human relationships. One such remark appeared very early in the book as Raskolnikov was about to make the acquaintance of Marmeladov, the incurable drunkard, as they sat in a dirty tavern. I quote from the translation I borrowed from the public library which I believe is superior to the text the school bought. 'There are some people who interest us immediately, at first glance, before a word is exchanged.' This is essentially how my interest in you began, almost from the very first time I sat in your class before a word passed between us. I am very content in your class. You are a very effective teacher. I don't think anyone would disagree with that.*"

"From now on," Dale promised, "when I get a letter, you get a letter. Can't we get Mortie in?"

Florence grimaced at the school psychologist's name. "Can you see Viktor with Mortie?"

"You've got to let his parents know he needs attention."

"I'll try." Florence's tone of voice, her shifting in her chair, taking in a glance the courtyard outside her office – a Japanese maple and forsythia in bloom, students smoking, necking, tossing a Frisbee – told Dale the opposite was true. The bell rang.

By June, the teacher had undergone a series of invasive tests and was told she couldn't conceive. Dale went to Florence's office with another thick Viktor envelope.

"Unprotected by you, I am prone to suicide. In place of a love of life I have substituted the next best thing: a virtuous person who loves life 100% of the time, this person being you. You supply the energy that protects me from suicide, so the extent of my dependence on you is clear. When I do get suicidal, I need something to make me hold on. I need something to make existence meaningful. I need you. When combined with trust, confidence, concern, and the willingness to return more help than is taken, need becomes 'entity love,' as I refer to it in my terminology. When love like this exists, those two involved are functions of one another, the existence of one guaranteeing the other, and the death of one necessitating the other's death as well.

"What is that? A threat on your life if you let him down?"

"I'm afraid so."

"Thank god summer intervenes."

Dale started to cry. "He's – like the twentieth century threatening annihilation if I can't make sense out of its break with the past."

The older woman put her palm over Dale's hand. "Or a troubled teenager trying to grow up."

The tears stopped. "Viktor thinks I can save him. He's a test I'm failing."

Florence beckoned Dale to the door and gestured. "In the Guidance Department, this is the time of year for tests and failures. At the end of June, we're concerned with averages, not specific exams, and whether you get the half credit to be promoted or graduate. Go see *Jaws* and put Viktor in perspective. We'll start over in the fall."

It was the worst of summers: letters from Viktor that Dale didn't open and hopeless, painfully repeated medical procedures. Then it was the best of summers: defeating Jimmy Connors, Arthur Ashe became the first black man to win a Wimbledon singles title. In late August, a positive lab test said Dale was due May first. She was saved.

Back at work in September, Dale felt Viktor was broken and she was not. He spooked her students by peering in at them with her. Then she received a note: "*My pessimistic fears are confirmed. I won't waste any of your time by recounting any of the dark suspicions I have. You don't want to hear from me. I accept that, no matter what the consequences may be.*"

Dale presented the note to Florence at the lunch table they shared in the teachers' cafeteria. Another teacher had Viktor as a new student.

"It's just September. I was getting around to seeing you, Flo," the man said, "The other kids don't want to sit near him."

"He's applied to Dale's alma mater," Florence sighed. "It's his only way of staying close to her."

"You can't let that mad boy go to college," Dale said. "I won't write a recommendation."

"He'll get accepted anyway," Florence said, noticing Dale's sleeveless blouse. "I'm the one supposed to be having hot flashes, not you."

"I'll be 98.6," Dale admitted, "for the next seven months."

Talk about Viktor Heinz was lost in pregnancy fanfare.

A month later, Viktor turned up at the literary magazine meeting. He sat silently while kids argued about how often they could publish their own stories and poems while leaving out everyone else's. Viktor waited for the meeting to end.

At the door, Dale said, "Viktor, let me be. I'm expecting a baby."

"You?" he cried and ran down the hall. It was after four p.m. on an autumn afternoon. Dale trudged to Florence's office, hoping she'd left, but her Department Chair was there. Together, he and Florence listened to the latest Viktor Heinz story.

"That's enough," the Chair said.

Viktor was absent the next day, and a weekend followed. On Monday, the Chair told Dale that after Friday's call from the principal, Viktor's parents had been relieved to have him hospitalized.

Viktor returned to school in November. He'd run away and refused further treatment. Florence reported he called psychiatrists 'illiterate and licentious'. Viktor took and received a perfect score on his SATs. He stayed away from Dale.

In December, Dale taught *Julius Caesar* to sophomores. In the years before video and then laptops in the classroom, students followed the text listening to a tape recording of the play. When Casca struck the first blow, the textbook Dale rested on her belly flew into an aisle, kicked by the fetal critic inside her. In April, a class broke school rules against parties by sneaking in a sheet cake, cartons of juice, and a ribboned bassinette filled with gifts. Except for the misogynist assistant principal who told her she was fat, and the poem Viktor submitted to the literary magazine right before the deadline, Dale was happy.

Dale read it and passed it on to her Chair. The poem was titled *The End.*

When my Lady says me nay,

my mountain fastness 'gins to sway;

I curse the night, I curse the day

my Lady turned from me away.

The mountain peak fuck-fingers God

Who shakes the climber from its peak –

O who'd with Lady only speak!

but ladies lure and gods betray.

The Principal said no and a storm started about it in the school newspaper, but the publication deadline passed, and all the students had read the poem, so the furor died as most springtime excitations did. Florence told Dale that Viktor had been accepted to the University of Chicago. Before Dale went on maternity leave in April, she frequented the faculty room bathroom between classes. There was Viktor, neatly dressed, thin and pale, blocking her way.

"I only wanted to be your friend," he said.

His eyes were dilated black. The winter-spring contrast of Viktor's narrow morbidity and Dale swollen fecundity was vivid. The faculty room door opened, and a math teacher emerged, assessing the scene.

"Everything okay?" he threatened.

Dale entered as her colleague exited, closing the door after her.

Over decades, when Dale thought of Viktor, it was never without a sense of fear and failure. She kept but never reread his letters. The Twin Towers that Dale had seen rise, fell. Another decade passed. In May, 2013, a spire capped the new 1776 foot tall One World Trade Center, and a coda to the old century came out of cyberspace: online in her alumni magazine, Dale read an obituary essay for her most influential professor at Chicago. It was written by Viktor, who at the university had become the protégé of the professor, a more apt Beatrice who guided him on to unknown others. A biographical squib identified Viktor's successful ongoing career as a partner, husband, and father, his sons attending Chicago.

In twenty-first century cyberspace, Dale and Viktor then 'associated' like subatomic particles. In response to her praise of his eulogy,

Viktor wrote familiar lengthy, laudatory messages. Dale tried delicately to describe their past entanglement to emphasize her relief at his survival. Viktor was repelled. He replied more recognizably, denying, accusing, and insulting her. Once again, he cast her as the evil Lady Who Said Him Nay. She read his denials as the brief of his life, written by the expert he had become. Dale found her Pinsky translation of Dante:

To get back up to the shining world from there
My guide and I went into that hidden tunnel;
And following its path, we took no care
To rest, but climbed: he first, then I – so far,
Through a round aperture I saw appear
Some of the beautiful things that Heaven bears,
Where we came forth, and once more saw the stars.

After Dale measured Viktor's fury against the griefs of decades past and yet to come, she still felt only relief: how Viktor or anyone escaped the levels of hell remained a mystery, but for the time being, Life had won! Hamlet's interim was enough.

Acknowledgements

The author thanks the editors of the following publications and presses, in which stories in this book first appeared, sometimes in earlier or different versions.

Alternating Current Arts for "Throw the Bones of Your Mother Behind You"
The Brooklyner for "Time and Tide"
Chiron Review for "Flash Gordon" (2011 Version)
Contexts South for "Eulogy for Miss Eulalie"
Footnote for "Throw the Bones of Your Mother Behind You"
Gone Lawn for "Gottesman's Constant"
Grey Sparrow for "Lives of Crime"
Inkapture for "The American Wing" (UK Publication)
The Kenyon Review for "Triptych" and "Flash Gordon" (1984 Version)
Per Contra for "The Man with Ten Hats" and "Viktor"
Persimmon Tree for "Mrs Dalloway Isn't Shallow"
Prick of the Spindle for "The Reckoning Ball" and "Manufactured Goods"
Red Ochre for "Viktor"
Review Americana for "Oberon"
Ryga for "The American Wing"
Tampa Review Online for "The End of the Cold War"
Tower Journal for "A Cultural Revolution"

L. Shapley Bassen's *The End of Shakespeare & Co.* was the winner of the 2009 Atlantic Pacific Press Drama Prize. She was a 2011 Flannery O'Connor Award finalist and is a fiction editor for prickofthe spindle.com. Ms. Bassen also won a Mary Robert Rinehart Fellowship for *German Sabbath*, which was published in 2014 as *Summer of the Long Knives*, about the successful assassination of Adolf Hitler. She has been published in numerous print and online publications, including *Kenyon Review* and *American Scholar*. She is a produced and published playwright and a commissioned co-author of a WWII memoir. A Vassar grad, she has been married for four decades and lives in Rhode Island.

www.ingramcontent.com/pod-product-compliance
Lightning Source LLC
Chambersburg PA
CBHW032148020726
47496CB00003B/765